Little Haunted Hall for Small Horrors

Ian Whybrow

Illustrated by Tony Ross

HAMNEEZIA

MT FAIRVIEW

GRIM MOUNTAINS

SKYWARD

MT. TESTER

BROKEN TOOTH CAVES

THE PARCHING PLAIN

DARK HILLS

BEAST

FRETTNIN FOREST

WINDY RIDGE

HAUNTED HALL

CUNNING COLLEGE
ADVENTURE ACADEMY

LAKE LEMMING

N
W — E
S

SCALE: 5 WINGFL

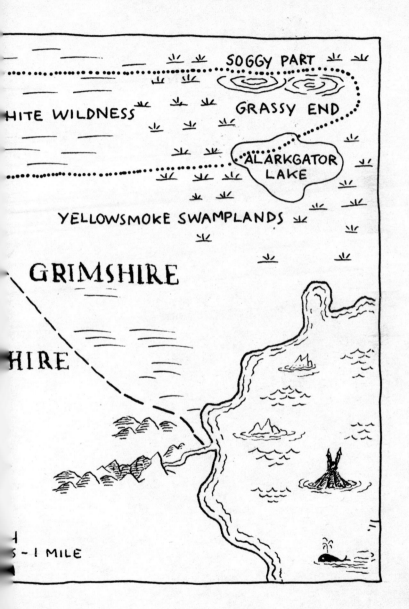

SOGGY PART

HITE WILDNESS   GRASSY END

AL'ARKGATOR
LAKE

YELLOWSMOKE SWAMPLANDS

GRIMSHIRE

HIRE

S - 1 MILE

HAUNTED HALL
FOR SMALL HORRORS

THE BEST SCHOOL
FOR BRUTE BEASTS

HUNTING AND HAUNTING OUR SPECIALITY

Heads: LW Wolf and Yeller Wolf
Caretaker and Fixy Boy: Stubbs Crow
Small Horror: Smellybreff Wolf
School Spirit and Spook: Mister Bigbad Wolf. R.I.P.

Dayschool lessons: Hunting for Gold,
Spooksuit making, Flying ect.
Nightschool lessons: Walking through Walls,
Shocking for beginners and all that
Playtime: Hello Ween and Midnight Feasts

HAUNTED HALL
FOR SMALL HORRORS

Dear Mum and Dad,

Please please PLEEEEZ don't be so grrrish. It's not fair Dad keeps saying, "GET A MOVE ON LAZYBONES, OPEN YOUR SCHOOL QUICK." Just because he has fangache, I bet, boo shame. Today I will do news 1st, then cheery pics for him after.

Yeller and me and Stubbs are trying and trying. Paws crossed we open soonly. But did you forget our 1 big problem I told you about before? I will tell you wunce more. It is the ghost of Uncle Bigbad. He is fine, in a dead way, but he keeps being ~~orkwood~~ nasty, saying do this and do that or no more haunting from me. Just because he knows we *neeeed* him for our School Spirit.

Here is a pic of Haunted Hall, the scaryest school in the world (opening soonly):

9

I am not drawing a pic of Uncle Bigbad.
Because 1) he is too crool, and 2) you cannot
see ghosts, only after midnight (get it?)

I will draw me and Yeller, my best friend and
cuz, instead:

ⓐ is just us being normal (Yeller is the loud 1).
ⓑ is us dressed up as bossy Heads saying, "No
chewing in class," ect.

Now I will do Stubbs the crowchick:

𝒶 is him being all proud of 2 new feathers.
𝒷 is him doing looptheloops in his glowmask.

And now just 1 more:
a Small Horror of
Haunted Hall in his
spooksuit. Guess who?
Yes, Smellybreff, my
baby bruv, going sob sob
I want my mummy. (Only
joking, he likes it here really.)

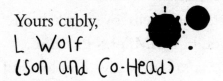

Yours cubly,
L Wolf
(son and Co-Head)

11

Dear Mum and Dad,

Your crool letter says my pics are soppy and cubbish. I only did them to make Dad's fang feel better. Why o Y is he so cross? Because I would not do a pic of his horrible dead bruv I bet.

So all right, here he is haunting our cellar in the night-time:

He only comes if he smells lovely bakebeans cooking in the pot. HMMM, YES PLEASE, SCOFF SCOFF. He says they give him loads of Spirit Force.

12

Mum says does he still look like Dad? Well, he looks just like before he died of the jumping beanbangs. Only now you can see through him. He has a big horrible furry face, plus big horrible red eyes, plus big horrible yellow teeth and all dribble dribbling down. Also his eyebrows meet in the middle like Dad's, only more caterpillery. Plus he is all green, also ~~loomy loominous~~ he glows in the dark. He is v fearsum plus he makes your fur stand up.

He likes to come slidingly through the wall saying a terrible WOOOOO! and GGGGRRRRAAAH! Also he likes saying terrible words like this:

I AM THE GHOST OF UNCLE BIGBAD!
ME WOT DIED OF THE JUMPING BEANBANGS!
I DROOL, I DROOL FOR A LUVLY GOBFUL!
FETCH ME THE SHOVEL AND FEED ME SWIFTLY!

But if you say, "Uncle would you like to be our School Spirit and teach our pupils your ghosty powers?" he says:

NO BLINKING BLUNKING FEAR,
2 MUCH LIKE HARD WORK.

Then he scoffs his bakebeans (canteen size) and off he vanishes.

Yours unhelpedly,
L Wolf (Head)

HAUNTED HALL
FOR SMALL HORRORS

Dear Mum and Dad,

Today Uncle said he *might* help us, but only if we hoover his grave. Also change the writing on his gravestone, boo shame, because it was good rhyming and true, saying:

> Bigbad Wolf
> is dead at last
> he died of eating
> beans too fast

Now he made us do:

> Dear Bigbad Wolf,
> We miss him so
> Do not be dead
> oh flip oh blow.
> M.I.P.

Yours wornoutly,

L

Dear Mum and Dad,

Posh new paper, eh?

Uncle appeared again for a scoff of bakebeans. He said, **"TELL ME (SLURP) WHAT STYLE OF SCHOOL YOU WISH TO OPEN. IF I LIKE THE SOUND OF IT (GLUP) I MAY POSSIBLY APPEAR IN IT, YOU NEVER KNOW. IF I HAVE NOTHING MORE PROMISING IN MY DIARY (WOFF)."**

So we said our ideas for him:

1) Me and Yeller are the Co-Heads, we can do all the Bossing About.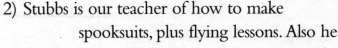

2) Stubbs is our teacher of how to make spooksuits, plus flying lessons. Also he is Caretaker and Fixy Boy with his clever beak. Plus he wants to be Bell Bird by flying up to the belltower and going ding on the bell (saves rope).

3) Smells is just a Small Horror (like normal, har har). Also his ted can be if he wants.

4) Our most important thing is loads of thrilly fun and laughs for all teachers and pupils.

5) Loads of midnight feasts of bakebeans (Uncle's best snack).

Uncle said, **"WOFF SCOFF, AND WHAT DO YOU EXPECT ME TO DO FOR YOU?"**

I said, "Uncle, Frettnin Forest is a fearsum place for small brute beasts. Thus and therefore it is v handy to learn What to Do if a Big Scary Thing Tries to Get You. Also their mums and dads want them to be Splendid Tuff Horrors. So will you be our School Spirit and maybe teach us some tricks and ghosty powers? Like Popping Up Quick and Hollow Larfing?

Uncle said, **"SNIFF SNUFF SNY, WHAT DO I SPY? I SPY FLIPPING FLOPPING HARD LABOUR! YOU WISH ME TO SHARE MY SPIRIT POWERS? AND BE A TAME TERROR TO TRAIN YOUR PUPILS? GRRRR, NO FEAR! I HATE SHARING. ALSO, I AM SO MIGHTY, YOUR SISSY PUPILS WOULD NEVER STAND UP TO THE SHOCK OF ME!!"**

Yeller said quick, "UNCLE, REALLY WE WANT YOU SHOWIN OFF YOUR POWERS, NOT SHARIN. ALSO, CAN'T YOU TURN YOUR TERROR DOWN A BIT?"

Uncle said, "HMMM, (GLUP) SHOWING OFF? YES, I DO LIKE THE SOUND OF THAT, I LOVE SHOWING OFF. YERSS. WELL P'RAPS AND MAYBE I WILL CONSIDER. BUT YOU MUST DOUBLE MY RATION OF (BURP) LOVELY BAKEBEANS, SO GOOD FOR MY SPIRIT FORCE. AND YOU CAN TIDY THIS BLINKING BLUNKING PLACE UP, IT'S A DISGRRRRRACE!"

20

Not fair,

Yours discustardly,
Little

ps You say what is M.I.P. on
uncle's new gravestone?
Answer, moan in peace.

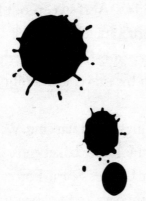

Dear Big bad Wolf,
we miss him so
Do not be dead
oh flip oh blow.
M.I.P.

Dear Mum and Dad,

Phew, work work work! Clean the blackboard, flit the flies, polish the desks, shoo the spiders, scrub the floors, windows and lavs. Also sweep out the cellar so it is posh enuf for Uncle's grate self to appear in. He is a big lazy ghost, also a greedyguts 2. He only does lying in his grave and scoffing.

Us worky boys are hungry and starving. We're not even allowed to eat the lovely bakebeans because they are only for Uncle's Spirit Force. We were saving them for rainy days and for being poor, like now, with no money from pupils, boo shame.

So please send rabbit rolls and mice pies.

Yours rumbletumly,
Littly

Dear Mum and Dad,

The rabbit rolls and mice pies were hmmmshus and yumshus. Yeller and me love them, kiss kiss. Smells saves all the tails and whiskers till last, then he eats them 2 quick and gets a coff – so cubbish! Also Stubbs says, "Ark," meaning thanks for the cheese, it was ark-stra spesh.

But why o Y do you say I have let the pack down being poor again? Because who put rockets under my safe and blew it up into small smithers? Who made my gold go raining all over Frettnin Forest so nobody can find it now? Answer, your darling baby pet, Smellybreff. But you never blame him, do you?

But now listen to *this* news, it is good. Yeller has just made up a fine advert saying:

23

ARRROOOO! Look out Richness, we are after you again!

Yours chestoutly,
L Wolf esqwire

Dear Mum and Dad,

Will you write and tell Smellybreff not to be a ~~noosink~~ ~~newsance~~ pain. Because me, Yeller and Stubbs are trying and trying to please Uncle to get him to be our School Spirit and Terror, and Smells keeps messing all our things up. Also we must rush about pantingly, pasting up adverts all over Frettnin Forest.

Tell him he must just muck around with his ted like a normal small bruv. Not keep asking to be a Co-Head like me and Yeller. Just because he got his Silver Daring Deed Award for Clues and

Courage when he was cubnapped by Mister Twister. But he is still 2 whiny and hopeless to play teachers proply. What do you think?

Your busywizzy boy,

L

PS How about a nice surprise for us, hint hint? Like some Ratflakes or Moosepops maybe?

HAUNTED HALL SCHOOL

FRETTNIN FOREST, BEASTSHIRE
HEADS: LITTLE WOLF AND YELLER WOLF ESQS
Deputy Head: Smellybreff Wolf Esq
CARETAKER: STUBBS CROW ARKSQWIRE

Dear Mum and Dad,

Thank you for your LOUD REPLY in red ink. Ooo-er. So yes, you're right, Smells must have his own way. Plus he can have a Deputy Head Badge if you want, plus be a Sir. Yes, I do remember he is your darling baby pet. And tell Dad yes, I do know what GOING RAVING MAD means, so no need him coming on a long journey to show me. Thank you wunce morely.

Yours toldoffly,

27

HAUNTED HALL SCHOOL

FRETTNIN FOREST, BEASTSHIRE
HEADS: LITTLE WOLF AND YELLER WOLF ESQS
DEPUTY HEAD: SMELLYBREFF WOLF ESQ
CARETAKER: STUBBS CROW ARKSQWIRE

Dear Mum and Dad,

    I said Smells could be our Deputy Head like you made me. But can you just tell him "No more caning people" and "Stop saying bend over swish all the time"?

Yours stungly,
    L Wolf (Head)

HAUNTED HALL SCHOOL

FRETTNIN FOREST, BEASTSHIRE
HEADS: LITTLE WOLF AND YELLER WOLF ESQS
DEPUTY HEAD: SMELLYBREFF WOLF ESQ
CARETAKER: STUBBS CROW ARKSQWIRE

Dear Mum and Dad,

Your photo of Dad saying PACK IN THAT CANING, PET arrived today. I showed it to Smells and guess what? It made him howl headoffly. Then he jumped in the cupboard and slam went the door.

I said to Yeller and Stubbs, "That was a good scare for him, he will stop hitting us now I bet."

Sad to say, he was just looking for some scissors. Now he has cut up your photo plus our curtains, tablecloff, ect.

Yours curtainlessly,
Little

29

HAUNTED HALL SCHOOL

FRETTNIN FOREST, BEASTSHIRE
HEADS: LITTLE WOLF AND YELLER WOLF ESQS
DEPUTY HEAD: SMELLYBREFF WOLF ESQ
CARETAKER: STUBBS CROW ARKSQWIRE

Dear Mum and Dad,

Good thing Smells found those scissors! He says Cutting Things Up is his best thing now. Plus Stubbs has trained him to do gluework. So now Smells says we must call him Mister Sticker and let him be a busy cub doing stickers all day. He likes footballers best, so lucky there are about 1 millium *Wolf Weekly Sports* in the shed for him to cut up and glue, eh?

Phew, now Yeller and me can do some proper thinking up ideas for our new scary school without *swish, ouch,* every time we bend over.

Yours cumfybottly,

L W

HAUNTED HALL SCHOOL

FRETTNIN FOREST, BEASTSHIRE
HEADS: LITTLE WOLF AND YELLER WOLF ESQS
DEPUTY HEAD: SMELLYBREFF WOLF ESQ
CARETAKER: STUBBS CROW ARKSQWIRE

Dear Mum and Dad,

Flip and blow. Putting up those adverts in Frettnin Forest was 2 days ago and still not 1 pupil has come. Y? I will say. It is because somebody has stuck Wanted posters all over them, that is Y! They are posters for Mister Twister the fox, saying:

WANTED
← MISTER TWISTER →
HE IS CUNNING,
HE IS NASTY
ALSO HE IS THE BEST
MASTER OF DISGUISE
IN BEASTSHIRE
—
BIG REWARD FOR CAPTURE

3 boos for a wopping, plopping fib! Because what about Uncle Bigbad? He is a lot more cunninger, crooler and worster. Also he is a brilliant dizgizzer if he tries his hardest. Plus he has loads of secret powers, I bet, only he hates sharing. Also he is 2 busy at the moment being a lazy loafer.

Yours insultedly,
Little

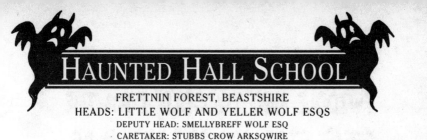

HAUNTED HALL SCHOOL

FRETTNIN FOREST, BEASTSHIRE
HEADS: LITTLE WOLF AND YELLER WOLF ESQS
DEPUTY HEAD: SMELLYBREFF WOLF ESQ
CARETAKER: STUBBS CROW ARKSQWIRE

Dear Mum and Dad,

Felt sad all day because Mister Twister's
Wanted posters made our adverts feel Unwanted.
But then Yeller had a brilliant idea! Make Uncle
a bit jealous! Because then maybe he will want
to show off and be more helping to us!

So at the bong of
midnight, when Uncle
came sniffsnuffingly after
his best snack (bakebeans,
canteen size), Yeller said
justwonderingly, "I WAS JUSTWONDERIN,
UNCLE, DO YOU THINK MISTER
TWISTER MIGHT GET A LOT
FAYMUSSER THAN YOU, WHAT WITH
YOU LYIN IN YOUR GRAVE MOST OF
THE TIME?"

33

Uncle said, "GRRRRR, THAT IS UTTER TWIDDLE AND TWODDLE. I AM THE GREAT STAR, FORMERLY KNOWN AS BIGBAD WOLF!! EVERYBODY KNOWS AND FEARS ME. I CAN DO FAR MORE CUNNING TRICKS THAN THAT MERE FOX! I CAN DO BUMPS IN THE NIGHT, I CAN DO WALKING THROUGH LUMPY OBJECTS, I CAN SMASH CHINA BY REMOTE CONTROL, I CAN DO GHASTLY HOWLS AND HOLLOW LARFS, NOT TO MENTION GOING HEADLESS AND OTHER MIGHTY SPIRIT POWERS LIKE FINDING LOST TREASURE."

Yeller said, "DID YOU SAY, 'FINDIN LOST TREASURE'?"

Uncle said, **"GRRRRR AND BLARST! DID I SAY MY POWER OF FINDING LOST TREASURE? YOU MADE THAT SLIP OUT BY MAKING ME JEALOUS, YOU BLINKING BLUNKERS! WELL, YOU CAN FORGET ABOUT ME SHARING THAT POWER! JUST GET BUSY! FETCH ME CROWDS OF ADMIRERS SWIFTLY, SWIFTLY. I DESERVE THEM, SO THAT I CAN THRILL AND AMAZE THEM WITH MY MIGHTYNESS!"**

Arrrooo! He is helpful to us at last! Must rush, new adverts needed!

Yours thinkythinkly,
Little

HAUNTED HALL SCHOOL

FRETTNIN FOREST, BEASTSHIRE
HEADS: LITTLE WOLF AND YELLER WOLF ESQS
DEPUTY HEAD: SMELLYBREFF WOLF ESQ
CARETAKER: STUBBS CROW ARKSQWIRE

Dear Mum and Dad,

Yeller and me did loads of new adverts. Phew, what a lot of drawing, also writing, colouring-in ect! All that work and no nice dinner after, boo shame (hint hint).

Stubbs did bring some chestnuts he collected from Frettnin Forest.

Yeller said all down and dumply, "THANKS, STUBBS, BUT WOLF CUBS DO NOT EAT PRICKLY CHESTNUCKS."

Stubbs said, "Ark Prrark," meaning they are not for eating, they are for prarktiss! He wanted us to go to the classroom and sit the chestnuts down at the desks. He said we could pretend they were hedgehogs adding up sums, then boss them about. Chestnuts do not put up their hands and call you sir, but true they are

36

v good for saying Headly things to, like "Tuck your shirt in, sonny."

Smells got jealous and says he is not Mister Sticker any more, he is Mister Woodcutter. So Stubbs made him a playcabin in the dining room. Also, Yeller let him borrow the chopper. Thus and therefore not much chairs and tables left, I fear. Maybe you want Smells back at The Lair quite soonly?

Yours beggingly,

Littly Wittly (snuggle snuggle)

PS This is a pic of what our larder is like (bare, get it?) Please send more grub: rabbit rolls, shredded shrews, moosepops, anything. Also something for Stubbs, and do you think you can find some tins of bakebeans (canteen size), we are getting short of them also, boo shame. Try looking for some in a cub scout camping place. But no eating them (the cub scouts, I mean) har har.

HAUNTED HALL SCHOOL

FRETTNIN FOREST, BEASTSHIRE
HEADS: LITTLE WOLF AND YELLER WOLF ESQS
DEPUTY HEAD: SMELLYBREFF WOLF ESQ
CARETAKER: STUBBS CROW ARKSQWIRE

Dear Mum and Dad,

Thanks for the grub. The Deerdrops, Moosepops and Ratflakes were lovely, also the Hamster Hoops and Goosabix. We like the packets 2, yum tasty! Stubbs says, "Ark," for the arkscellent Maggot Mix. No bakebeans? Pity. (Don't tell Uncle only a few left.)

We have put up our
new adverts in Frettnin
Forest. Paws crossed there
are no more Wanted
Mister Twister posters to
cover them up, eh?

I am writing my quietest and most notdisturbly
because Yeller is making up something clever.
A Kwestion Hare I think it is called. It is not an
advert, it is a new way to tempt the mums and
dads of Frettnin Forest to send small brute beasts
to Haunted Hall. Also it is going to mention
about our Entrance Test (our
test to get in, get it?)

Arrroooo, Yeller's ideas
are just the best! Because
the mums and dads will say
to their small brutes, "Oh
goodie, a test for you, and you
are such a brilliant cheater."

Yours mercybucketly,
moi (French)

39

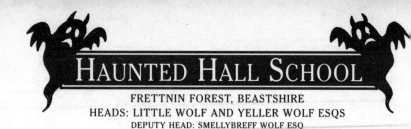

HAUNTED HALL SCHOOL

FRETTNIN FOREST, BEASTSHIRE
HEADS: LITTLE WOLF AND YELLER WOLF ESQS
DEPUTY HEAD: SMELLYBREFF WOLF ESQ
CARETAKER: STUBBS CROW ARKSQWIRE

Dear Mum and Dad,

At sunjump today, Stubbs went highflying to drop Yeller's Kwestion Hares all over the forest. Paws crossed for many a reply. By the way, Yeller says maybe some parents can pay in bakebeans instead of fees, good, eh? Because that will help keep Uncle a happy haunter.

I'm sending 1 Kwestion Hare for you to see. A bit smudjy, sorry, Smells did a spit on it (jealous), also Yeller's writing is a bit hilly.

Yours rushly,

Little

40

KWESTION HARE
ABOUT HAUNTED HALL
* ? * ? * ? * ? * ? *

IMPORTANT KWESTIONS FOR PROUD
PARENTS FROM L AND Y WOLF, CO-HEADS,
HAUNTED HALL SCHOOL, FRETTNIN FOREST
(DO YOUR TOOTHMARK OR TICK IN 1 BOX
ONLY)

CAN YOU READ? (TRICK QUESTION)
YES ☐   NO ☐   MY BRANE IS 2 SMAL ☐

HAVE YOU GOT MONEY FOR FEES (NOT FOR
FLEAS)
YES LOADS ☐
NO WE ARE A BIT SAD & POOR ☐

IF NO MONEY, WILL YOU PAY IN
BAKEBEANS?
NO ☐   YES, BIG TINFULLS ☐

IS YOUR CUB, PUP, FLEDGIE ECT JUST A
WEAKY?
YES ☐   NO ☐

DO YOU WANT HIM LEARNIN TUFFNESS OR
JUST CURLIN UP OR HIDIN DOWN HOLES?
TUFF ☐   CURL UP ☐   HOLE HIDER ☐

DO YOU WANT HIM LEARNIN GOOD
HAUNTY POWERS AND SURVIVAL TRICKS
OFF OF A PROPER GHOST SUCH AS BIGBAD
WOLF OR JUST NORMAL BORIN LESSONS?
HAUNTIN AND TRICKS ☐   BORIN STUFF ☐

DO YOU WANT HIM BEIN A HORROR OF
HAUNTED HALL OR JUST GOING TO A
RUBBISH SCHOOL?
HAUNTED HALL, THE BEST SCARYEST
SCHOOL IN THE WORLD ☐   ANY OLD DUMP ☐

WILL YOUR SMALL BRUTE COME FOR OUR
ENTRANCE TEST?
PROBLY ☐   DEFFNLY ☐   MAYBE ☐

IN A SHORT WAY, SAY WHAT HE/SHE/IT
NEEDS TEACHIN MOST (ANSWER IN BEST
PICS OR WRITIN, NO PAWPRINTS)

HAUNTED HALL SCHOOL

FRETTNIN FOREST, BEASTSHIRE
HEADS: LITTLE WOLF AND YELLER WOLF ESQS
DEPUTY HEAD: SMELLYBREFF WOLF ESQ
CARETAKER: STUBBS CROW ARKSQWIRE

Dear Mum and Dad,

ARRROOOO!!

Stubbs just flew in the window with a Kwestion Hare filled in by a dad weasel! He has ticked the YES LOADS OF MONEY box (arrroooo x 3!) Also he likes the look of Haunted Hall. Look at his answer to SAY WHAT HE/SHE/IT NEEDS TEACHIN MOST:

Our pup Throttler is a blot on the family, he has gonn veggie. We will pay big munny if you be strict teachers and teach him back to being a propper bludthirsty weasly boy aggin.

43

Plus he has ticked the DEFFNLY box for doing the Entrance Test! Just wait till Uncle hears, he will go thrill thrill I bet.

Yours zestfully,
Littly

HAUNTED HALL SCHOOL

FRETTNIN FOREST, BEASTSHIRE
HEADS: LITTLE WOLF AND YELLER WOLF ESQS
DEPUTY HEAD: SMELLYBREFF WOLF ESQ
CARETAKER: STUBBS CROW ARKSQWIRE

Dear Mum and Dad,

I am all upset. I did not know wolfs are sposed to look down on weasels. But Uncle says they are common riffraff and much 2 easy to impress.

He says, **"YOU SEEM TO BE FORGETTING THAT I AM THE STAR ATTRACTION AND TERROR AROUND HERE! I DEMAND A BETTER CLASS OF CREATURE TO PRAISE MY SPLENDIDNESS."**

45

Oh boo, now Uncle says no more public appearances from him. Also no helping with Entrance Tests unless 1) we promise xtra helpings of bakebeans from now on, and 2) we gloom the place up a bit.

He says 2) is to remind him of his lovely grave, but really he is only letting off his spite. Just because we just finished getting HH all neat and cheery I bet!

Yours sinkingly,
Little

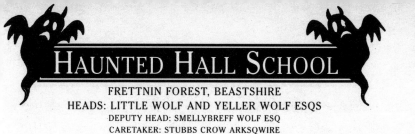

HAUNTED HALL SCHOOL

FRETTNIN FOREST, BEASTSHIRE
HEADS: LITTLE WOLF AND YELLER WOLF ESQS
DEPUTY HEAD: SMELLYBREFF WOLF ESQ
CARETAKER: STUBBS CROW ARKSQWIRE

Dear Mum and Dad,

Phew, just time for a short note because of working and working to make the place more gloomish. No more electric for us – Uncle says candles are heaps better for shivery shadows.

1 good thing has happened from this. Smells has stopped being Mister Woodcutter (lucky, because yesterday he unmade 6 beds in the dorm going chipchop with his chopper).

Now candles are his best thing and he wants us to call him Mister Waxworks. Because he chews candles up all soft and makes models. So far he has made just blobs but he calls them faymus stars off the telly, footballers, ect. Such a simple dimp.

Yours grownupply,
L Wolf

HAUNTED HALL SCHOOL

FRETTNIN FOREST, BEASTSHIRE
HEADS: LITTLE WOLF AND YELLER WOLF ESQS
DEPUTY HEAD: SMELLYBREFF WOLF ESQ
CARETAKER: STUBBS CROW ARKSQWIRE

Dear Mum and Dad,

So nice today! You would not *beleeev* how many answers to Kwestion Hares Stubbs has flown in. Lots of them say YES to paying large fees just for the chance to learn tuffness tricks and ghosty powers off us and Uncle!

Yeller is just back from a spider hunt. He has got buckets of fat tickly 1s, brilliant for making nice sticky webs plus hiding lurkingly down plugholes, inkwells, ect.

Stubbs helped me do a fine banner for waving from our flagpole on the belltower, saying:

HAUNTED HALL ENTRANCE TEST
This Sat at Ghosty time
Be there and have a good scare

Also we have done a fine job putting *eee-aaahs* in the doors. Next we must do some *creeeeks* in the floor, plus make all the radiators go *blugblug ticktap* in the night. Uncle will be all swole up with proudness I bet. So he will probly say:

GRRRR, I AM SO PLEASED I WILL SHOW YOU YOU MY POWER OF FINDING LOST TREASURE!

Smells is doing car alarm noises. He thinks it helps.

Yours deffly,
Little

HAUNTED HALL SCHOOL

FRETTNIN FOREST, BEASTSHIRE
HEADS: LITTLE WOLF AND YELLER WOLF ESQS
DEPUTY HEAD: SMELLYBREFF WOLF ESQ
CARETAKER: STUBBS CROW ARKSQWIRE

Dear Mum and Dad,

Everything is ready for Entrance Test Day nearly, only 2 nights to go now.

Yeller has made the cellar a more dungeonish smell with old cabbage water plus poking cheesefur into cracks.

I went on a spooky chain hunt but not much luck. Just the 1s off our bikes, so not clanky enuff. BUT (big but) I have made all our family portraits of Uncles, Grandads ect a lot better. By putting swivelly eyes in them, they follow you round the room. Good, eh? My next job is make some

50

secret panels so we can play Hide and Skweak.
Get it?

Stubbs's clever beak has got Smells busy!
Because, guess what? He made 2 Action-cub
battlesuits, 1 is for him, 1 is for his ted. Also he
put up the tent in the back garden. Arrroooo!
Now Smells can live *outside* so not being in our
way! He can chew his candles and make his
waxworks plus do car alarm noises all he likes.
Also going, "Bangbang, Mister Mozzy,
Bangbang, Mister Ant, I got you, you are
dead." ect.

Yours muchbetterly,

Little

NeeeeNaaaa!

HAUNTED HALL SCHOOL

FRETTNIN FOREST, BEASTSHIRE
HEADS: LITTLE WOLF AND YELLER WOLF ESQS
DEPUTY HEAD: SMELLYBREFF WOLF ESQ
CARETAKER: STUBBS CROW ARKSQWIRE

Dear Mum and Dad,

Tomorrow night is the night. *Crowds* of brutes are coming, so Uncle can have a good show off and we can have loads of fun. Stubbs is here saying, "Ark," meaning send a few arksamples, so I am.

Arksample 1, a small tortoise is coming. His mum thinks he is 2 shy so he needs a good shocking to get him a bit more out of his shell.

Arksample 2, Mister Webfoot is sending a jamjarfull of his frogspawn jellydots from the pond up by Lake Lemming. He thinks a scary school will help turn them into tadpoles.

52

Nextly, 3 fraidy bats. Their dad is fed up of buying nightlights and says can we get them used to the dark?

Plus Mrs Rattlesnake wants a lot of strictness for her young Squirmer. Because he has a bad habit of sucking his rattle and it gets 2 soggy.

Plus *loads* more have filled in our KHs. Also Smells has captured 6 bugs and insects that came creepingly to his tent. [He made a mini waxworks Chamber of Horrors on a tray to attract them. Then he went har har gotcha and popped them in his matchbox.]

Yours hummingly,
    Mmm mm (guess who)

HAUNTED HALL SCHOOL

FRETTNIN FOREST, BEASTSHIRE
HEADS: LITTLE WOLF AND YELLER WOLF ESQS
DEPUTY HEAD: SMELLYBREFF WOLF ESQ
CARETAKER: STUBBS CROW ARKSQWIRE

Dear Mum and Dad,

Here is 1 of our Entrance Test papers for you to see:

ENTRANCE TEST PAPER FOR HAUNTED HALL SCHOOL

TASK 1:
Sit quietly in the dark and wait for a ghost to pop out. No lickwashes, no scratching, no chewing test papers.

TASK 2:
When ghost comes, do your loudest WOO!

54

TASK 3:
See how quick you can dig a hole with an Entrance to it. Pop down it. Say, "Well done me, I have passed my Entrance, that was an easy test! Now I can be a pupil and give heaps of my dad's riches to Haunted Hall!"

TASK 4:
Pop back, then draw a nice pic of our Haunted Hall ghost.

TASK 5:
Learn the Haunted Hall School Song and sing fortissimo (your head off.) This is it:

we are the Horrors of Haunted Hall
Spooky are we, we are not scared at all
No matter how tuff other brute beasts are
we are more crafty so nah nah nah!

Do you like it? Now we are all ready and Uncle 2. We have said to him do not forget to appear just on the bong of midnight tomorrow night like normal. Only *do not be 2 scary* because remember 2 much jitters might make small brutes run away from Haunted Hall.

I am sure he will not appear 2 harshly. Because he promised, saying:

WHO ME? WOULD I?

Yours trustingly,

L

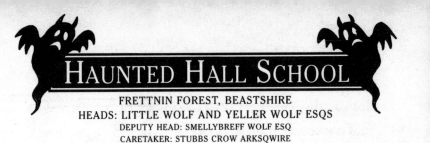

HAUNTED HALL SCHOOL

FRETTNIN FOREST, BEASTSHIRE
HEADS: LITTLE WOLF AND YELLER WOLF ESQS
DEPUTY HEAD: SMELLYBREFF WOLF ESQ
CARETAKER: STUBBS CROW ARKSQWIRE

Dear Mum and Dad,

I am all upset. Our Entrance Test was so good but then Smells and Uncle letted us down.

Such a big long line we had outside the front gate! And that was only just after the sun hid. By midnight, phew, what a wopping big crowd!

So Yeller and me did our Headly looks, saying (stern voices), "All hold hands in 2s, quickmarch and sit up straight in nice rows in the cellar." Also Stubbs did everso good caretaking. He did pulling the blinds down, mopping up sicks plus taking wrigglers to the toilets.

We let Smells stir the bakebeans in the pot, also give out some Test papers. Then guess what he went and did? He opened his matchbox up and said to his captured bugs and insects, "Hello,

57

I am Mister Sticker," then he glued them to the fridge.

That made all the other pupils go jumping about saying, "Help it's a trap! Help save me from being a fridge sticker!" ect.

Yeller said, "OO-ER, LET'S HOPE UNCLE REMEMBERS NOT TO BE 2 SCARY. SMELLS HAS MADE THESE PUPILS A BIT NERVOUS."

Up went the lovely steam of bakebeans, tempt tempt, from the pot. Then BONG came midnight. And all of a suddenly, right on time, Uncle appeared.

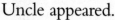

But he did not even *try* not to be 2 scary!
He did not come like a normal ghost
at all. He came in going

CRACKLE
FIZZ
FUME
FLASH!!

Because he was dressed
up as a big raging
forest fire!!!

From your feeless boy,
L Wolf

HAUNTED HALL SCHOOL

FRETTNIN FOREST, BEASTSHIRE
HEADS: LITTLE WOLF AND YELLER WOLF ESQS
DEPUTY HEAD: SMELLYBREFF WOLF ESQ
CARETAKER: STUBBS CROW ARKSQWIRE

Dear Mum and Dad,

Did I say about all our small pupils running
away very very very very swiftly? Well, then Uncle
said, **"GRRRAAA HAR HAR, WASN'T I
FANTASTIC, THE WAY I MADE ALL
THOSE SHINY PINK LITTLE
BEASTS GO CHARGING
BACK TO THEIR HOLES?"**

Yeller replied, "THEY WEREN'T PINK
WHEN THEY CAME IN, THAT WAS ONLY
BECAUSE YOU SHOCKED THEM OUT OF
THEIR SKINS! LOOK AT ALL THESE
LICKLE FURRY SUITS LYIN ABOUT ON
THE FLOOR.
NOW WE SHALL
HAVE TO POST

THEM ALL BACK TO THEIR MUMS AND
DADS. AND NOT ALL OF THEM HAVE
GOT THEIR NAMES SEWN IN."

Uncle just larfed his hollow larf, saying,

"HOOO HAR HAR, I HAVEN'T HAD
SUCH A GOOD TIME SINCE I DEVOURED
THE POSTMAN! BUT NOW TELL ME
HONESTLY, WASN'T I JUST TERRIFYING
AS A FOREST FIRE? DIDN'T YOU JUST
LOVE THE WAY I FRIGHTENED
THAT SKINNY GREY YOUNG
FELLOW? I MADE HIM
GO SCUTTLING
UP THE CHIMNEY!"

I said, "Uncle, he was just a small shy tortoise.
You were sposed to bring him out of his shell
gently. But no, you made him go out pingingly
like a wet soap. It will take us ages fitting him

61

back in. And what about the Red Admiral butterfly you shocked into a Cabbage White?"

Uncle said, **"ANOTHER MASTERSTROKE! YES, I BELIEVE THAT HAPPENED WHEN I TRANSFORMED MYSELF INTO A PACK OF HOUNDS. CONGRATULATE ME SWIFTLY SWIFTLY ON THAT SPLENDIDLY DARK POWER! THAT WAS THE FIRST TIME I HAVE TRIED DIVIDING MYSELF AND BARKING IN MANY PLACES. MOST EFFECTIVE, WASN'T I? THANK YOU, THANK YOU!"**

I said, "But Uncle, you *promised* to appear gently. Those dark powers you did were 2 harsh."

Uncle said, **"STOP WHINING, VILE FLUFFBALL, YOU ARE GETTING ON MY**

NERVES, SPOILING MY HORRID FUN! AND I WANT MORE! THOSE LITTLE SQUEAKERS WERE FAR TOO EASY TO SCARE! THEY ARE A WASTE OF GOOD TERROR. SO NOW YOU MUST HAVE A BET WITH ME."

I said, "What sort of a bet, Uncle?"

He said, "I BET YOU MY POWER OF FINDING LOST TREASURE THAT YOU CAN'T FETCH ME ANY BRUTE BIG ENOUGH OR BRAVE ENOUGH TO STAND UP TO ME DOING MY DARKEST AND DIRTIEST. SHALL WE SAY FOR 5 MINUTES?"

Yeller said, "BUT THAT IS A HARD BET FOR US. WHAT IF WE LOSE?"

Uncle said, "TUFF! IF YOU LOSE, I SHALL GO ALL SULKY AND NOT HELP YOU AT

ALL, AND THAT WILL SERVE YOU RIGHT FOR MAKING ME WORK SO HARD. I SHALL RETURN TO MY GRAVE FOREVER AND HAVE A WELL-DESERVED M.I.P.!"

I said, "But how can we have a Haunted Hall School without you?"

Uncle said, "EXACTLY! NOW BE SILENT, SPECK! I WILL GIVE YOU 3 TURNS OF THE MOON TO SEARCH, NO MORE. GRRRAH HAR HAR!"

Oh dear, Uncle is such a teaser.

Yours headscratchingly,

L

HAUNTED HALL SCHOOL

FRETTNIN FOREST, BEASTSHIRE
HEADS: LITTLE WOLF AND YELLER WOLF ESQS
DEPUTY HEAD: SMELLYBREFF WOLF ESQ
CARETAKER: STUBBS CROW ARKSQWIRE

The larder

Dear Mum and Dad,

Help! We have looked and looked in every
hole and hollow tree in Frettnin Forest and not
1 brute is brave enuff to stand up to Uncle's
powers. So now I must travel MILES afar to find
such a rufftuff creature.

Yeller wants to come with me but I said no,
Smells needs looking after. Also he must guard
the school in case of robbers.

Uncle is horrid and lazy. Last night he could
not be bothered going back to his grave even. He
has moved into 1 of his old whisky bottles he
found in the larder. Just because of it saying
'Powerful Spirit' on the label. He said:

65

So vain.

I must go to our library and look up Tuff Creatures.

Yours studyingly,

L

HAUNTED HALL SCHOOL

FRETTNIN FOREST, BEASTSHIRE
HEADS: LITTLE WOLF AND YELLER WOLF ESQS
DEPUTY HEAD: SMELLYBREFF WOLF ESQ
CARETAKER: STUBBS CROW ARKSQWIRE

The library

Dear Mum and Dad,

Cor, encyclopeeeeeeedias are fat, did you know that? They are so heavy you have to use both paws for holding and get Stubbs to sit on your head and turn the pages for you with his clever beak. Pity he is left-beaked because it made him start from Z and work backwards, so it took ages to get to A. And, oh no, A was just the letter we wanted for a rufftuff reptile!

67

Stubbs went, "Ark! Alark!!" meaning A is for Alarkgator!

Oo-er, so now I must find 1 and bring it back to win the bet against Uncle, save Haunted Hall School and discover the power to find my lost gold. But sad to say the nearest alarkgator lives many a mile away in Yellowsmoke Swamplands. That is in Grimshire! How can I get there, and back with an alarkgator, in just 3 turns of the moon? Yellowsmoke Swamplands takes 7 turns of the moon to run there and back, maybe 8!

Yours stumpedly,

HAUNTED HALL SCHOOL

FRETTNIN FOREST, BEASTSHIRE
HEADS: LITTLE WOLF AND YELLER WOLF ESQS
DEPUTY HEAD: SMELLYBREFF WOLF ESQ
CARETAKER: STUBBS CROW ARKSQWIRE

The dorm

Dear Mum and Dad,

Cannot sleep. Yeller has got paper all over the floor. He is scratching and scratching planningly with his pen. But 2 late I fear. Stubbs also is a busy widewaker. He is doing knitting plus making something from 1 of Yeller's inky plans. I do not know what, but there is canvas in it, also tentpoles, string, plus Yeller's kite with the wolf eyes on.

I think maybe they are both just taking their minds off us being poor and starving for ever. Because not even Yeller can think up a brilliant way to get to Yellowsmoke Swamplands AND come back with an alarkgator by Wensdie (cannot spell it).

Yours failedly,
Little

69

HAUNTED HALL SCHOOL

FRETTNIN FOREST, BEASTSHIRE
HEADS: LITTLE WOLF AND YELLER WOLF ESQS
DEPUTY HEAD: SMELLYBREFF WOLF ESQ
CARETAKER: STUBBS CROW ARKSQWIRE

Under tree in front garden

Dear Mum and Dad,

Something gulpish. Are you ready? Gulp.
Stubbs says he wants to *fly* me to seek for an
alarkgator!

He says, "Ark!" meaning Arkshun Stations!
Also he says two new tail feathers have come, so
his flying is strong.

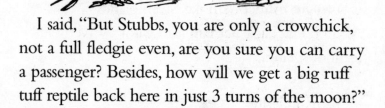

I said, "But Stubbs, you are only a crowchick,
not a full fledgie even, are you sure you can carry
a passenger? Besides, how will we get a big ruff
tuff reptile back here in just 3 turns of the moon?"

He just says, "Ark!" meaning do not worry, he is an arkspert at flying now. Also he has made a thing from Yeller's plan that is a secret invention to help us. But no time to arksplain now.

Yeller is a bit upset not to come, but he must stay and do guarding in case of robbers, plus being minder of Smells.

Our crunchy snacks are packed and I just put on my string harness that Stubbs knitted. We are ready. I just want to say a small message for my grave in case of emerjuncy:

Here lies L. Wolf
He fell off the sky
He was a bit 2 heavy
but never mind,
good try.

Your trembly boy,
Little

Dear Mum and Dad,

Sorry about the scribbul, this is a flying airletter. We are up. Aayee, I love highuppness it is so thrilly, kiss kiss! The wind takes your breff and pins your ears and fur back. Stubbs is a strong airswimmer but getting bit tired now. Frettnin Forest is like moss below.

Now we are over the Parching Plain. It is bumpy. Stubbs says, "Ark!" meaning arkstra hot air because of the burning sands. So bouncy.

Poor Stubbs, I think he has got the

Wing

a
c
h
e

Dear Mum and Dad,

We did a crashland, a dusty 1, but our bones
stayed together. Lucky us, eh? So hot here,
phew! I am trying to make a shadow so Stubbs
can sleep cool and get his strongness up. I
wanted to read about Yeller's invention. There
is a paper with it called 'Instruckshuns', but my
head is busy having thinks. Are there some tuff
and fearless brutes that live in parching plains?
Maybe, and then no need to fly further, eh?

My thinks are up in the sky above now. I can
hear buzzards saying *keeee-keeee* in case we are a
nice snack for them. Oo-er, I remember now,
buzzards are v fierce with hooks for claws, also
sharp beaks. Ding! An idea has just jumped in
my head! I will play dead and try to capture 1
when it comes down to eat me.

Yours backsoonly (I hope),
    Little Snack (just kidding)

Dear Mum and Dad,

Cor, I did not like that buzzard coming up close. I made my eyes slits but I saw him looking at my tasty parts. So I said, "'Scuse me, I am just a small beakful and my friend here is also. P'raps you would like to come back with us and meet my Uncle. He is a lot bigger."

The buzzard said, "Kee-keee! How big is hee-ee?"

I said, "Very big, p'raps you have heard of him, his name is BB Wolf."

And do you know what?
Off he went, *VOOOM*. Such a
big softy. Lucky the wind of him
voooming made Stubbs nice and cool.
He is feeling a lot better!

Yours Readyfortakeoffly,
   Little

Dear Mum and Dad,

Brr, Broken Tooth Caves and Grim
Mountains far under us. Can see roofs small as
sparrownests, Hamneezia maybe. So frozz up
here now. Stubbs is flapping very hard. I must
stop writing and make myself streamliney.

Yours cheeks suckedinly,
Little

Dear Mum and Dad,

Oo-er, I fell asleep for a bit. When I woke up I thought, "Oh no, I have turned into a polar bear cub sitting on a big seagull!" But do not fret and frown, it was just us flying through a blizzard.

1 good thing, it will be a soft crash if we do fall because the White Wildness is all snow. But paws crossed Stubbs can keep going as the crow flies, eh?

Yours fridgly,
Brittle (joke)

76

Dear Mum and Dad,

Phew, landed
hardly at
Yellowsmoke
Swamplands,
but not
crashingly
because of
swamp. But
now a bit mucky.
Stubbs is my hero.

We are trying out Yeller's new invention – a
Tentyglider, it's brilliant! The Instruckshuns are
quite hard, but if you fold it 1 way you can do
camping in it (the door is Yeller's kite with the
yellow wolf eyes on). And if you fold it a new
way, it turns into a glider. So Stubbs can tow
even wopping grate brutes in it!

Camping out is my worst thing, even with
Stubbs for company. Bad things happen in the

night. Like you hear the bogeywolf coming up the stairs to get you. He goes *step step step step step*. Then you wake up and you think, phew, no stairs in here, it was just a squirrel plopping nuts onto the roof.

More later from,

Yours widerwakely,
Little

Yellowsmoke Swamplands, up the grassy end

Dear Mum and Dad,

Later. No alarkgators yet, but we did find a lion. He was hiding in the long grass. Stubbs was upset because he had feathers on his tongue, so we did not go 2 near.

I shouted out to him a 'scuse me, saying, "Hmm, I do not 'spect you ever get scared, do you?"

He said, "SSPITTT RRRUMBLE GGRRRAAA! RRRRidiculous idea!"

But when I said about coming with us to our cellar to stand up to Uncle Bigbad's shocking powers for 5 minutes he said, "Er, d'you mean Bigbad Wolf? Oh, dribbly feller, very bad temper? Um, well you see, I must have my wide open spaces. Otherwise I would come with you and do my bit for the Pride, I honestly would. But cellars, no no, much too closed in, you follow me? And no lovely long grasses to tickle my tummy. Goodbye." Then he ran away.

Getting darkly dim now, but still, Mum always says: *Yellow eyes are friends with the dark.* So handy about our yellow wolf-eye door which is nice and scary. Also lucky our camp is on an island (they are safe from sharp teeth). Wish we had some islands in Frettnin Forest.

Yours yawnly plus an "Ark" from Stubbs,
Little

80

Dear Mum and Dad,

You want to be careful about islands. Because sometimes they are alarkgators. And when you get up in the morning, better not go, "Hmm, breakfast, yum." Just in case your island starts thinking breakfast thoughts 2.

Also, if you see a sort of green bridge going up in front of your eyes, do not walk across, it might be the alarkgator opening his mouth. Better if you stay where you are on his back and say, "Good thing I put this tent up on you because cor, it makes you look so hansum." (Rule 3 of Badness, fib your head off.)

I did hear a funny *vrroomba vrroomba* in my ear in the night, but 2 tired and cosy to get wurrid. Then this morning I found out the alarkgator just ate a small cub that was listening to his Walkwolf. That is Y his words have got a beat, like, "Jump in my pool, it's really cool."

I said, "Hello, I am L Wolf Esqwire and this is S Crow Arksqwire. We are here to tell you about a nice prize you have won in a raffle. It is a trip on a glider to visit a funny school. Would you like to come?" (More Rule 3.)

The alarkgator said:
"You don't fool me with your talk about a raffle ha!
Get in my jaws and let me snaffle ya!"

I said, "You are very rufftuff. Are you scared of anybody? Like a wolf maybe?"

The alarkgator said:
"My name is Snap, I am where it's at
I'm a cool cool alligator.
I am the jaw you can't ignore
Catch you now, or catch you later!

Hope you don't mind if I say to you
You'd be mighty good to chew.
You look tasty, you look crunchy
How would you like to be my lunchy?"

I said, "Oh, all right." Because I remembered another 1 of Mum's best sayings, the 1 about how to get untangled if you are in a prickly bush. She always says: *You must give to the blackberry bush before he'll let you go.* So I held Stubbs by the wing and we jumped in the alarkgator's mouth. And guess what I gave him? Answer, the tentpole!

Arrroooo! He lashed and splashed and splashed and lashed but he *could* not eat me and Stubbs for his lunchy, har har.

Yours unchewedly,
Little

Dear Mum and Dad,

Do you know what? That alarkgator was just a big baby! He cried and cried just because me and Stubbs tricked him with the tentpole and he could not eat us. So no good us gliding *him* back to HH to stand up to Uncle, because he would probly say "Boohoo blub" straight away, then Uncle would win his bet, boo shame.

Now me and Stubbs are all glim and glumly. Because 2 turns of the moon have gone already! We had a chat and we said shame, Grimshire is a bit rubbish, better go back to Beastshire. So Stubbs said, "Ark!" meaning arkay with him.

He had to fly us back across The White
Wildness, then over Mount Tester to Broken
Tooth Caves. So hard for him, but on and on he
flew flappingly with no moaning. Also we hit
the land gentle as a leaf.

Sometimes you get outlaws here but I 'spect
we will not see any. We have made the
Tentyglider into a glider just in case. Now off we
go into the caves with our torches going flash.

Yours searchingly,

L

Dear Mum and Dad,

No luck finding outlaws but guess what?
A Mountain Ranger has come to help us. He
has got sharp eyes, a pointy face and a smell like
pepper. His uniform is nice but sticky out at
the back.

He spoke softly to us
saying, "You look like
smart young chappies
and I have some
questions for you. Will
you gaze into my eyes
and answer them?"

We did not know how to say no to him. So
we said all about searching for a large brute that
is not afraid of a certain faymus terror. He said,
"My boys, you interest me strangely. Am I to
understand that you are referring to that terrible
crook and miser, Bigbad Wolf? Him, as they say,
'wot died of the jumping beanbangs'."

86

I said a proud, "Yes," and Stubbs said, "Ark," meaning I arkgree with Little.

The Ranger said, "Amazing! What is his racket now?"

I said, "He does not play tennis, he is a shocking ghost and master of spirit dizgizzes. Also Star Attraction at Haunted Hall, the scaryest school in the world."

The Ranger said, "And where exactly is his residence?"

I said, "He has a v nice grave, but just lately he has moved into a whisky bottle in the larder at Haunted Hall. But when us 2 can find a beast that is not scared of him for 5 minutes, he will say by Spirit Power where all my gold is hiding. So I will be rich wunce morely."

Then the Ranger got very peppery, and he said that was *very* interesting. Now, arrroooo, he says he knows a way to help us! Because he knows a brute beast that is not scared of *anything*. All we have got to do is go with him to the edge of a very steep cliff and wink down his telescope.

Good, I hate steepness, but I like telescopes. More later.

Your nosy boy,
Little

Dear Mum and Dad,

Sorry about the nervous writing, there is a bear, it is big

(behind us).

yrs goodbyfreverly,
L Wolf

Bears' camp near a fast river, Dark Hills, Beastshire

Dear Mum and Dad,

Oh no, we are captured by bears, and it's all that Ranger's fault!

We were on a path just a small way down from the top of a

s

t

e

e

p cliff.

The Ranger said for us to look peepingly through the telescope at a boy and girl cub. They were standing in a roary river, fishing for salmon. You would not *beleeeev* how strong they are for cubs! Also they gave each other such fierce bites and cuffs! The mum bear was there but she was 2 busy scoffing honeycakes to watch them.

That Ranger was silly. He would not be still! He kept standing up so the sun went flash on his shiny buttons. Also he kept doing loud coffs.

I said, "You want to be careful, this path is thin. Just spose a huge big brute comes up behind, there is only room for 1 of us to escape quick!"

That was when Stubbs went, "Ark! Ick!" meaning arkscape quick! Because the dad bear (wopping huge) was right behind us holding my tail in a tight squeeze. And guess who escaped quick? (Clue, not me or Stubbs.) Answer, the Ranger!

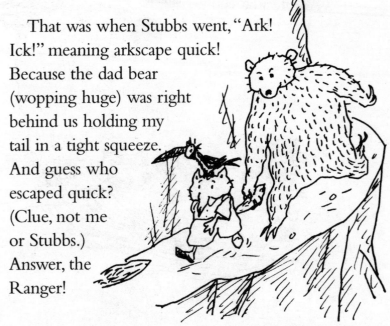

But just then came a loud scream. Stubbs shouted, "Ark!" meaning arkcident. The boy cub got swept away by the roary river. Quick as a chick I said to the bear, "Let go my tail and we will save your cub." So he did.

Now I know, Dad, you will say, "Why o Y are you still captured? Y not flee away quick and say 'Har har I was fibbing my head off'?" Answer, we need that cub!

Yours daringdeedly,
Little

Dear Mum and Dad,

The boy cub nearly got drownded in the rapids. But Stubbs dropped me on him in the water with Yeller's strong kite string tied to my harness. I bited hold of the fur on the bear cub's neck. Then Stubbs gave the other end of the string to the dad bear. Even the lazy mum bear stopped scoffing and came to pull.

The dad and mum bear pulled and pulled, then PLOP, out of the roary water we came.

The dad bear whacked the boy bear 2 good 1s, saying, "THAT's for being stupid and THAT's for next time." Then the mum bear whacked him a hard 1 also. Then the girl cub bit him, then he bit her back. And do you know what he said? He said, "Rocks and rapids can't scare me! I like banging my head on rocks! I did that on purpose, so there!" And he gave me a hard push out of the way and climbed up a tall tall tree.

93

His mum said, "Get down out of that tree, Normus! There are bees in that nest, they'll sting you all over!"

The boy cub said, "Bees don't scare me, I like getting stinged." Then he got stings in his nose plus on his black tongue even and he just said, "Har har, doesn't hurt!"

It did really, he was just showing off. Also he threw the hive at me for a joke to make the bees chase me.

That is Y I said we need that bear. He is a big bully, but I think he can win the bet against Uncle! I just hope his mum and dad will let him go with me and Stubbs.

Yours hopingly,
Little

Dear Mum and Dad,

I think the Bears have got more nasty tempers than Dad. (Not really, only kidding Dad, yours is the baddest.) So it was quite easy to take Normus away from them. Because he gets on their nerves a lot. Also they say they do not know what to do with him. Maybe that is Y they did not eat me, plus they liked listening about me being a wolf cub, also a proud Co-Head of Haunted Hall School.

Mr Bear said to me, "So you're a wolf cub and he's a crowchick, eh? Funny that, because I thought maybe you was just somethink wot the cat coffed up! And you're starting up a school, you say? Now I don't see that. I don't see you being a teacher at all. Wot I see is you covered in honey and spread on my sandwich. Unless you can prove you ain't telling me big fat fibs!"

Quick as a chick I said, "Pay attention, claws on lips, come along come along!" like we did for practiss on the chestnuts.

Mrs Bear said, "Oo, he knows all the sayings, just like a proper teacher! Do some more!"

I said, "Now then, sit up straight, no chewing."

She said, "Oo, ain't he luvly? Go on, Dad bear, let's send Normus away to his school. After all, he never learns nuffink off of us, does he?"

Dad bear said, "How do we know it's a proper strict school with the right sort of School Spirit and all that?"

I said, "Haunted Hall has got the strictest most shockingest School Spirit in Beastshire. His name is BB Wolf."

Dad bear said, "Well that's all right then. And do you believe in short sharp shocks?"

I said, "Oh yes."

Dad bear said, "Good. Just what he needs. The only way to get sense into him is to knock it in. So don't take no cheek off of him. Show him the back of your paw. And a good sharp bite never does him no harm. Does it, Normus?"

But Normus wasn't listening. He was wrestling with his sister for a tin of peaches (canteen size). He grabbed it off her and opened it. Sideways. With his claws. Oo-er.

Stubbs has finished putting the glider together. Hope Normus does not break it with his strongness.

Yours pawscrossedly,

Shore of Lake Lemming, night of the 3rd moon

Dear Mum and Dad,

Such hard flying for Stubbs! He had me in
the harness plus towing the glider behind. Phew,
what a shouter that Normus is. Nearly loud as
Yeller. He kept shouting, "Higher higher!
Gliding can't scare me!"

It was dark 2, also some cold rain spit.

Over Windy Ridge flapped Stubbs. The air
was so bumpy and frozz, it was like a fight all the
way to Lake Lemming. We were a bit wurrid
when we got there, about no runway. Also all
the dark trees on the edge of Frettnin Forest.

But good old Yeller. He was thinking of us in
the night. He did not want us going bash into a
tree. So he said to Smells, "QUICK MISTER

WAXWORKS!
RUN TO THE
SHORE OF THE
LAKE WITH YOUR
CANDLES AND YOUR
SHOVEL! WE MUST MAKE
2 TONS OF MOLEHILLS
AND PUT LIGHTS ON THEM."

That made a nice landing place and
down went Stubbs and the glider behind
with Normus on it, all smooth and crashless.

Stubbs and me did 3 arrrooooos for joy and
said, "Well done and thanks, Yeller and Smells!"
But not Normus. He just gave Yeller a
Chinese burn, saying, "Flying can't scare
me! I like crashing!" Then
he said to Smells, "Hello,
Stickybud, let's
play Head in
Mouth, bags
you go 1st!"

Smells did not stay. He gave Normus 1 of his nasty looks. Then he took the shovel and ran off quick as a chick to his tent in the back garden.

I said to Normus, "No time for rufftuff games, we must hurry to school before midnight OR ELSE."

He just said, "OR ELSE *what*? Can't make me. Teachers can't scare me."

I said, "Good thing 2. Plus I hope you are not scared of Uncle Bigbad either!"

Yours wishmeluckly,
Little

HAUNTED HALL SCHOOL
FRETTNIN FOREST, BEASTSHIRE
HEADS: LITTLE WOLF AND YELLER WOLF ESQS
DEPUTY HEAD: SMELLYBREFF WOLF ESQ
CARETAKER: STUBBS CROW ARKSQWIRE

Dear Mum and Dad,

Back we went rushingly to Haunted Hall.
We needed to hot up bakebeans in a pot quick.

Haunted Hall was all glum and glim and
gloomy, but Normus did not seem to be 1 bit
nervous. He just kept barging us saying, "Let's
have a wrestle," ect, also getting in our way a lot.

Then Stubbs said, "Ark!" meaning hark, the
bong of midnight! But Normus did not be still.
He pulled a big bunch of nice new feathers
out of Stubbs's tail. Such a big bully!

Then all of a suddenly,
Uncle came swooshingly
out of his whisky bottle,
more glowy and horrible
than before even.

101

He did Hollow Larfs plus Terrible Screams,
then some new Terrible Words:

**SNIFF SNUFF SNARE, I SMELL BEAR!!
SNIFF SNUFF SNUP, I WILL EAT HIM UP!!**

Normus went a bit quiet. But then he said,
"Ghosts can't scare me! I'm a *big* bear, I like shocks!"

So Uncle went, **"RRRRRAAAAAARRRR!"**
And he did his Forest Fire and his Pack of
Hounds and his Swarm of Killer Bees.

But Normus just said, "Can't scare me, I can be nasty like that, look!" And he gave 3 hard kicks, 1 for me, 1 for Yeller, 1 for Stubbs. Then he sat on us. V hardly.

Uncle said, **"HOO HAR HAR, I KNEW IT! HE'S BLINKING BLUNKING TERRIFIED OF ME."**

But he wasn't really.

Yours squashedly, **Little**

HAUNTED HALL SCHOOL

FRETTNIN FOREST, BEASTSHIRE
HEADS: LITTLE WOLF AND YELLER WOLF ESQS
DEPUTY HEAD: SMELLYBREFF WOLF ESQ
CARETAKER: STUBBS CROW ARKSQWIRE

Dear Mum and Dad,

What a big cheater Uncle is! I wrote a
message on the back of a stamp and posted it in
his whisky bottle for him to read. It said:

Hmm hmm Uncle,
you have lost your
bet. Normus is not
scared of you a
bit. Now you must
teach us your power
of finding lost
gold ect.

Then out came his ghosty voice saying,

"GRRRRAAAAH, LAST NIGHT DOES NOT COUNT, I WAS NOT EVEN TRYING TO BE A TERROR, BUT JUST YOU WAIT! TONIGHT I SHALL SCARE THE BEAR'S FUR OFF!!"

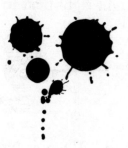

Oh boo, I forgot Rule of Badness number 9: NEVER trust a big bad wolf.

Yours cheatedly,
Silly me

HAUNTED HALL SCHOOL

FRETTNIN FOREST, BEASTSHIRE
HEADS: LITTLE WOLF AND YELLER WOLF ESQS
DEPUTY HEAD: SMELLYBREFF WOLF ESQ
CARETAKER: STUBBS CROW ARKSQWIRE

Dear Mum and Dad,

Oo-er, Uncle was so scary in the night! He did The Crawling Paw. He made the paw go creepingly up the wall by itself outside the dorm window. Then it went *scritch scratch* with its nails. It made me call out, "Oo-er, help! Where are you, Stubbs and Yeller?" But no need to ask because I found out all of a suddenly they were tucked up tight right next to me!

Then I said, "Where is Normus?" Answer, fast asleep. Not 1 bit nervous even. Ah, but then he had to get up to go to the loo. The dark was deep and the floorboards did *ee-arrs*. We held our breaths waiting for a big shock. Then Normus pulled the chain and we heard:

"SSSSHHHHHHAAAAAAH"!

Har har, that was Uncle
jumping out of the
toilet being a Terror!

But Normus just
went back to bed
yawningly. He did not
bother to light a candle even. Also before he got
back in bed he went donk on our heads with
the toilet brush saying, "That's for you becuz I
hate your toilet. But toilets can't scare me, so
there!"

Yours lumply,
Little

HAUNTED HALL SCHOOL

FRETTNIN FOREST, BEASTSHIRE
HEADS: LITTLE WOLF AND YELLER WOLF ESQS
DEPUTY HEAD: SMELLYBREFF WOLF ESQ
CARETAKER: STUBBS CROW ARKSQWIRE

Dear Mum and Dad,

Hope you can read this, I am see-through (Yeller and Stubbs 2!) So maybe my ink is also! Shall I say how? Answer, training by Uncle in secret powers!

He has really got his temper up now. I was having a small zizz on the table-tennis table. It was still daytime, not near Uncle's haunting hours. But he broke the ghost rule and came out of his bottle to give me a message. He was 2 cross 2 stand still so he dressed up as a pingpong ball and used me as a net. He said:

Now I will tell you about Uncle's training. It's easy cheesy! All you do is hold on to a ghost's tail. Then his powers run through you (all tickly) and you can stay see-through till the 1st cockodoodle of the dawning.

You can go 1-2-3 Pop! And off comes your head. Or you can do a little hop and up you go floatingly like a small cloud. Hmm, nice feeling.

So in the deep dark, Uncle whispered, "FOLLOW ME." Up we went floatingly through the ceiling of the dorm going "WOO!" We went through all the beds, furniture ect, plus we made all Normus' bedclothes go walking round him. And our best thing was turning into small skeletons. Because then we got in the biscuit tin by Normus' bed and did a very noisy tapdance, har har!

Normus jumped out of bed. Not because of terror, oh no. He said, "Spooks and skellingtons can't scare me. I am tuff, I am ruff. Now I am going outside to bash up Smellybreff!"

What can we do to stop him?

Yours triedeverythingly,
    L Wolf

PS. Uncle is no help, he just says TUFF. Sorry.

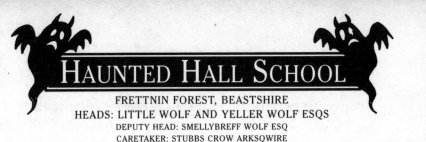

HAUNTED HALL SCHOOL

FRETTNIN FOREST, BEASTSHIRE
HEADS: LITTLE WOLF AND YELLER WOLF ESQS
DEPUTY HEAD: SMELLYBREFF WOLF ESQ
CARETAKER: STUBBS CROW ARKSQWIRE

Dear Mum and Dad,

Did you think to yourself hmm, I was
wondering Y Smells took that shovel when he
ran off? Me 2. Answer, he went to his tent with
it for digging a bear trap! So he did not get
bashed after all, arrroooo.

We all peeped over the edge. Normus was
down nice and deep. He saw us peeping and
said, "Traps can't scare me. I will get out any
minute, then I will bite you hard."

Yeller said, "TRUE. PLUS HE WILL
SQUASH US AGAIN I BET. QUICK LET'S
GET ALL STRICT!"

111

Stubbs said, "Ark! Wark!" meaning yes he is so arkward he deserves a hard whack. Also Smells wanted to be Mister Hunter and donk him with his chopper.

But I said, "No, no more bashing."

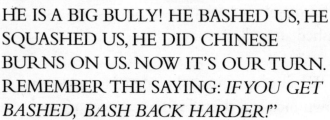

Yeller said, "BUT Y NOT? HE IS A BIG BULLY! HE BASHED US, HE SQUASHED US, HE DID CHINESE BURNS ON US. NOW IT'S OUR TURN. REMEMBER THE SAYING: *IF YOU GET BASHED, BASH BACK HARDER!*"

I said, "But everybody bashes Normus. It doesn't do any good. His mum bashes him, his dad bashes him, even his sister bashes him."

Stubbs said, "Ark! Shark!" meaning he needs a short sharp shock, he pulled out my best feathers!

I said, "No more bashing, no more shocks, no

112

more strictness. This is what we'll do." I did an important whisper to all the chums and off they went thinkingly to work.

Then I said down the bear trap, "Normus, are you listening? We are going to fetch a ladder to let you up."

Normus just said, "Good, becuz then I can squash your heads in."

Yours oo-erly,
Little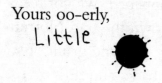

HAUNTED HALL SCHOOL

FRETTNIN FOREST, BEASTSHIRE
HEADS: LITTLE WOLF AND YELLER WOLF ESQS
DEPUTY HEAD: SMELLYBREFF WOLF ESQ
CARETAKER: STUBBS CROW ARKSQWIRE

Dear Mum and Dad,

Da-daaah! Just in case you thought oh no our boy is killed dead by a head squash, here I am again.

Because listen what happened. We got ready, then we put the ladder down the trap. Normus started climbing up going grrr and grufff. I said, "Normus, have you ever had a chum?"

He said, "Wot's a chum?"

I said, "You know, a friend, or somebody that likes you and only does pretend bites."

Normus said, "No, I haven't got 1, everybody hates me."

114

I said, "Aha, that was *before*. This is *after*. So come out now and have your surprise."

Normus said, "I know surprises, they are donks on my head!"

I said, "No, no donking. Listen, I like you, Yeller likes you, Stubbs likes you. You have won a bet and now we will be rich because you are the only brute beast in Beastshire with the braveness to stand up to Uncle Bigbad."

Yeller held out a stiff paper with all writing on in nice colours done by him, saying, "NORMUS BEAR, I PRESENT YOU WITH A STIFFKIT OF BRAVENESS. WELL DONE. AND BECAUSE YOUR READING IS A BIT RUBBISH, I WILL SAY THE WORDS FOR YOU."

Then he read:

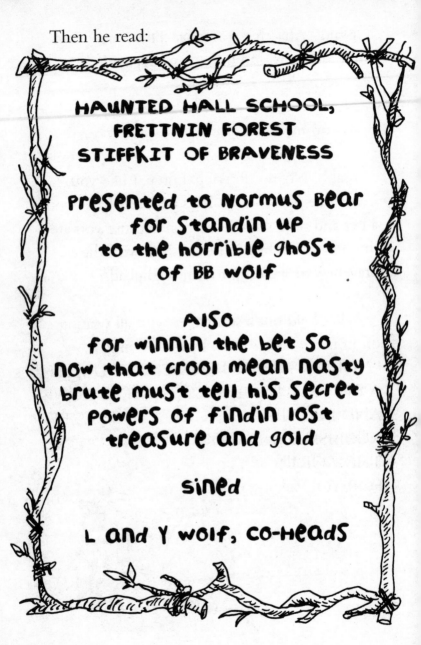

HAUNTED HALL SCHOOL,
FRETTNIN FOREST
STIFFKIT OF BRAVENESS

presented to Normus Bear
for standin up
to the horrible ghost
of BB Wolf

Also
for winnin the bet so
now that crool mean nasty
brute must tell his secret
powers of findin lost
treasure and gold

sined

L and Y Wolf, co-heads

Normus said, "You mean, you really like *me*. Even the crow? Even that small diggy cub with the shovel?"

I said, "Well, not Smells, no. He hates everybody. But the rest of us."

A big tear fell off Normus' nose and he said, "This is the best, most scaryest school I know. I'm not going home. Ever. I want to stay and have chums."

And we said all right then, you can be our 1st proper pupil. Then Stubbs flew up to the belltower and gave the bell a hard ding for Haunted Hall's 1st proper daytime lesson: Spooksuit Making.

Yours proudly,
L Wolf Esqwire
(Co-Head)

HAUNTED HALL SCHOOL

FRETTNIN FOREST, BEASTSHIRE
HEADS: LITTLE WOLF AND YELLER WOLF ESQ
DEPUTY HEAD: SMELLYBREFF WOLF ESQ
CARETAKER: STUBBS CROW ARKSQWIRE

Normal Boring School

Dear Mum and Dad,

Big shock! We took Normus into the larder
to meet Uncle in his whisky bottle, also to say
come on, be a sport, pay up your bet. But oh
no, a burglar has been and done stealing! It was
while we were all in the back garden. And guess
what he ~~burglard~~ ~~stealed~~ ~~burguled~~ pinched?
Answer, the whisky bottle!

Oh boo, now we will never find out the
power of finding lost treasure. Also, that is the
end of Haunted Hall. Because the burglar has got
the 'haunted' part, in other words, Uncle! Boo
shame, because Normus will probly think we are
now just a normal boring school and go home.

Yours startagainly,
L

118

Dear Mum and Dad,

Thank you for your LOUD LETTER saying about the shame of losing our best relative. You say will he ever Moan in Peace again? Also you say I have let down the name of the pack, so Dad has gone all sulkish. He says he will not come and visit us here *ever*, not till his lost bruv is back in his happy haunting ground.

OK, I will try my hardest to do hunting for that burglar. Off I trot.

Yours scentingly,
Little the tracker

Dear Mum and Dad,

All I have found so far is 1 will-of-the-whisker down the marshy end of the forest. Also 2 bad pongs, but sad to say made by skunks, not Uncle. Yeller came and found me. He has not found Uncle either. He says Smells is all upset. He took the stuffing out of his ted to look, in case Uncle was hiding in there, but no luck. Now, just because he put the stuffing back wrong, he says Yeller stealed ted and left behind a fat tortoise.

Stubbs says he will help restuff ted proply, but
not just yet. Because when he was highflying
about looking down owlholes he bonked into a
branch. So a sore beak for Stubbs too, boo
shame. Plus Normus got his head wedged in a
tin of peaches. Maybe he thought Uncle wanted
a bath in peach juice.

Will we ever find Uncle's trail?

Yours lipnibblingly,
Little

Dear Mum and Dad,

As I said, no luck yesterday, but today everybody went round the house clueing with magnifying glasses plus notebooks and sharp pencils. We got v tired and v feddup. But by teatime, bit by bit, everybody found maybe 1 small cluelet:

Smells found 1 foxy pawprint (found in rosebed outside larder window).

Normus found 2 red whiskers.

Stubbs found 1 toggle off of a Ranger's jacket.

Yeller found 1 nose smudge on a custardskin in the larder.

And I found 1 Ranger's hat that made me sneezy.

122

Add them all up and they = 1 greedy Ranger with red whiskers and a smell like pepper that knows about Uncle Bigbad's power of finding lost treasure.

I said, "Hmm, let me think. That is just like the Mountain Ranger who let me get captured by Normus' dad! He was peppery. Also I noticed his coat was bulgy at the back. Oo-er! Now I know who that was! He was not a Ranger at all. He was that Wanted crook and Master of Dizgizzes (cannot spell it), MISTER TWISTER!"

Yours,

Sherlock Wolf (get it?)

HAUNTED HALL SCHOOL

FREETNIN FOREST, BEASTSHIRE
HEADS: LITTLE WOLF AND YELLER WOLF ESQS
DEPUTY HEAD: SMELLYBREFF WOLF ESQ
CARETAKER: STUBBS CROW ARKSQWIRE

The Yelloweyes Forest Detective Agency

Dear Mum and Dad,

Normus says clue hunts are his best game ever and never mind about Haunted Hall closing but can he be in our pack? He likes being our chum but also he wants to be a detective. Good, eh?

So from now on we are all going to do solving crimes and mysteries all over the forest. So no more schools, no more horrors, no more Haunted Hall.

We are The Yelloweyes Forest Detectives!

THE YELLOWEYES FOREST DETECTIVE AGENCY

Detectives: LW Wolf and Yeller Wolf
Flying Squad: Stubbs Crow
Large Clue Hunter: Normus Bear
Small Clue Hunter: Smellybreff Wolf

Tracking Tricking Dizgizzing
our Speciality

So look out you big robbers and crooks like Mister Twister. The YFDA is on your trail!

Yours elementary-my-dear-mum-and-dadly,
L Wolf, Forest Detective

[French]

Little Wolf,
Forest Detective

Ian Whybrow
Illustrated by Tony Ross

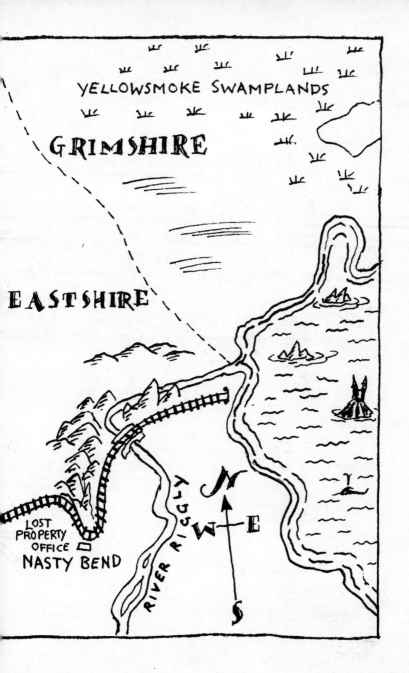

(Not Haunted Hall School any more, hem hem Mister Postman)

The Office with the big desk in

Dear Mum and Dad,

Please please please PLEEEZ don't make me come home to Murkshire to live in the Lair with you and Smells. Why o Y can't I stay here in Frettnin Forest with Yeller, Stubbs and Normus? Because we like being detectives, it is good. Stubbs has made us posh badges with his clever beak like this saying YFDA (for Yelloweyes Forest Detective Agency, did you know that?).

Also on our door he has done a nice new ~~sing sine~~ notice saying:

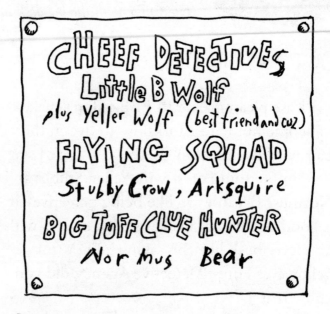

CHEEF DETECTIVES
Little B Wolf
plus Yeller Wolf (best friend and cuz)
FLYING SQUAD
Stubby Crow, Arksquire
BIG TUFF CLUE HUNTER
Nor mus Bear

We are good solvers but not Smells. His brane is 2 small plus he did not want to be in the YFDA. He got all feddup and lairsick remember? That is Y he came back to Murkshire to live in the Lair with you, then he could be your darling baby pet, yes? So not my fault.

Go on, make him stay there, we do not want him back, messing up our detective stuff. Like sitting on the fingerprint pad and doing bottomprints on my notebook. Also, he is selfish saying nobody else can be the handcuffer, only him.

Go on.

Yours hopingly,

Little Wolf

My room

Dear Mum and Dad,

You did not say much to my last letter, only hmmph and grrrr, and where is Uncle Bigbad's ghost? Find him quick or else!!!

We have been looking and looking, only no luck yet. Still, I have done you nice pics of what's in our detective kit so you will get more cheery. Yeller sent off for it to *Wolf Weekly* (cheap). It is like this:

DETECTIVE KIT

Magnifying glass

Pawprint set

Handcuffs

Detective Notebook with stickers like *INTERVIEW NOTES* and *CLUE NOTES* and *EVIDENCE* and *THINKY OUT PAGE ect.*

Sharp pencil with earclip

Torch to help yellow eyes see in the dark

Penknife for sharp work

By the way, you say what new cases have we got to solve, grrrr? Answer, allsorts but confidenshul, privat, can't say anything hem hem.

Yours acely,

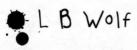 L B Wolf

Co-Cheef Detective, YFDA

Dear Mamong et Parp-parp (french),

No we have not found Mister Twister yet. Yes, I do remember he has shamed the name of Wolf by being a kidnapper and ghostnapping Uncle Bigbad in his whisky bottle. But do not fret and frown, we will solve this case soonly, easy cheesy. (Probly.) But just now we are a bit busy doing Tips for Tecs to help us. Do you like them?

TIPS FOR FOREST TECS

- *practise magnifying, pawprinting, handcuffing, sharpening (pencils) and shortpaw writing*

- *Use your brute instinct*

- *Use your keen beastly senses, such as eyes, ears, nose, also having a good lick*

- *Find clues*

- *Write about them in your notebook quick but no smudjis*

- *Have a good think*

- *Do plans for fast getaways*

Then you will be Mister ACE Forest Detective and case solver, arrroooo!

Good, eh?

Yours cheefly,

L Wolf (son)

Dear Mum and Dad,

You keep saying what is the point of being your son if I do not blab my secret cases to my mum and dad? Oh OK then, I will say about just 1, but keep it in the Lair. It is called The Case of the Ants' Lost Football Boots. Now I will say about the solving part.

The captain of Ants United FC came under our office door wearing his captain's strip with his number on (Number 9999999). He said antly, "Hello, somebody has pinched all my team's football boots, can you detect who dunnit?" Normus said, "Yes and I will bash them up for you." But me and Yeller and Stubbs said, "No need for bashing, Normus. Just adding up, plus using your keen beastly senses."

12

So Normus said, "Right then, how many boots got pinched?" and the captain said, "All the lot." That was a hard sum to add up, because of ants having to times by loads of feet. But Yeller got the answer, 6 x 11= 66. Then Normus said to the ant, "Hoy, have you got any reserves?"

Good thing he said that because the answer was yes, 1. That made 72 boots pinched. And guess what? We solved who the stealer was! Arrroooo for the YFDA!

And now:

NEW MYSTERY CRIMES OF FRETTNIN FOREST

1) 13 pups, chicks, cubs, fledgies ect. have gone missing from Frettnin Forest in 2 days

2) Also much treasure keeps getting robbed

3) Reports coming in of strange spookly small things seen in the night

Good. Because that means loads more detecting for us. So watch out all you kidnappers and robberers and small spookles, because we have a detective kit and we can find out WHODUNNIT!

Yours trackingly,

L B Wolf

Co-cheef Detective, YFDA

Under dinner table (for cosyness, hmmm)

Dear Mum and Dad,

About *The Case of the Ants' Lost Football Boots*, I forgot to finish off, sorry. The solving part was, we got out our magnifying glasses and had a good look round the heap where the ants live, going stare stare.

Anycase, quite soonly, we found many a small track. We followed these, crawlingly, to a rotted log. And guess what we found hiding under the bark? A centipede wearing 72 football boots! Stubbs can speak Insect so he said, "Ark Squark Crark?" ect. meaning arkscuse me, small crook, are you warking for Mister Twister the Farks? Or are you warking alone as a stealer? Also have you seen the ghost of Bigbad Wolf in a whisky bottle by any small chance?

The centipede said (insect voice), "It is a fair cop, misters. But I have not seen a big bad ghost and no I do not work for Mister Twister. Also, I am not a crook really. I just wanted to do loud riverdancing and get faymuss. By the way I taste horrible, hint hint."

Then he tried to do a fast getaway but no, he tripped over his laces and got captured har har. So well done us.

Yours Xplainingly

Littly

PS He Xcaped soonly, boo shame. Must get smaller handcuffs.

Dear Mum and Dad,

We had a good wet hunt for Mister Twister and Uncle Bigbad's ghost today, so I bet you are going pat pat well done our cub. Yeller's Big Ideer was to swim down and look at Lake Lemming's bottom. Because you never know, Mister Twister is crafty enuff to hide down there. We saw some nice bubbles, also Normus caught a nice fishy tea (yum yum tasty). But no crooks or ghosts in whisky bottles, boo shame.

17

The ants' football team came over today saying we can be best friends and they will give us a kick-about any time. Good, eh? Also, today we got a hansum reward because we found a lost froghopper in the long grass and took him back to his mum. She was so happy, she gave us some cuckoo spit. So now we have got some nice froth to go on cups of hot choclit, yum yum tasty!

Yours yawnly,

Laaah Waaaah Zzzzzz

Dear Mum and Dad,

It is not my fault Smells is jealous of my adventures. He always gets jealous. So go on, make him stay with you, hmmm? stroke stroke. Also, you are not fair, saying grrrrr you bet we do not earn much money being detectives because we cannot find my own dead uncle even. True we are not rich yet, BUT (big but) what about all that gold I had in my safe till Smellybreff got some gunpowder and blew it to small smithers? That made my gold go scattering all over Frettnin Forest.

Never mind, guess what? Stubbs found 3 gold coins high up in some nests yesterday! Arrrooo! So well done our Flying Squad, good searching.

19

Now I will tell you a bit more about what wants solving.

KIDNAPS

The Case of the Small Missing Moose
The Case of the 3 Bunnies that Hopped it
The Case of the 4 Pinched Hedgepiglets
The Case of the Lost Lion Cub
The Case of the 4 Disappeared Ducklings, ect.

Also

ROBBINGS

The Case of the Jackdaw's Jewels
The Case of the Weasel's Gold Watch

SPOOKLY HAUNTINGS

The Case of the Green Bubble that Floats in the Night-time

Oo-er! What is happening? Where have the small brute beasts all gone? Who pinched the jewels and the watch? What comes floating about in the night like a green bubble? Do not fear and fret, do not get wurrid, the YFDA will soon find out. Arrrroooo!

Yours yellow-eyedly,

Little

PS Mum always says yellow eyes are friends with the dark, yes? So look out clues, we are after you even with all the lights out.

Sulking corner

Dear Mum and Dad,

Thank you for your harsh letter saying we are not proper detectives but you know somebody who is.

You say this somebody is not called a detective, but a Private Investigator which is a lot more posh. And he told you magnifying glasses are rubbish. He has got all hi-tech tools for detecting and he is called Furlock Homes-Wolf. And he is faymuss because he solved *The Hard Case of the Slippery Chicks*.

Now I feel all jealous.

Yours unpraisedly,

L Wolf

My desk (tidy 1 with all sharp pencils pointing same way)

Dear Mum and Dad,

Very busy work today using brute instinct and beastly senses. Today I will copy out some pages from our notebooks so you can say, hmm, nice detecting you cubs.

YFDA INTERVIEW NOTES
(Privat keep out smells or else)

Case 1

TIME

early

DETECTIVE ON CASE

N Bear

TIME OF INTERVIEW

Just after sun jumped up.

WITNESS STATEMENT OF

Mrs Duck, Tidynest, The Reeds, Lake Lemming (up the deepend).

"I was bobbing up and down counting my babies like you do. I never seen feather nor beak of nobody, only that nice gingery man with a mask on his face and a sort of fur badge on his front. He was holding a bag of crumbs. Then I noticed all my fluffies was gorn. Gorn! Oh woe is me, ect."

PLAN

Normus will go hunting, in Lake Lemming area, for gingery man with mask on (bit suspish) plus furry badge also 4 small ducks with fluff on.

Case 2

DETECTIVE ON CASE

Yeller Wolf

TIME OF INTERVIEW

Just after snacktime

WITNESS STATEMENT OF

Mr and Mrs Lion,
Anywhere we feel like, Parching Plain.

"A travelling knifegrrrinder with squinty eyes came pushing his grrrrinder

over our hunting grrround. We noticed
he was wearing a fur brrrrooch and he
smelled minty. He said he had a special
offer on claw sharrrpening, so we
thought why not? It was just after he
went that we noticed our small cub was
not asleep in his patch of long grrrrass.
We rrreckon he was cubnapped."

Yeller to Parching Plain to track
suspect pushing minty knifegrinder with
fur brooch. Also looking for kidnapped
cub called Pounce (left ear chewed).

Case 3

DETECTIVE ON CASE

S Crow

TIME OF INTERVIEW

Ark past 2

WITNESS STATEMENT OF

Mrs Hedgehog, Heapoleaves,
Beech Grove, Frettnin Forest.

"A gingery gypsy it was. Selling clothes
pegs with big spots. On her hanky.

She had a spotty hanky, you understand, see? Her clothes pegs were not spotty, right? I noticed she smelled minty and she had a fur thingy pinned to her blouse. Is that a help?

Snuffle snuffle. Excuse me. I am upset. I am always telling my hogglets never to take slugs from a stranger! But it was just too tempting for my little cheeky chestnuts. Now they have been torn from me. You must find them for me Mister Defective. I will pay anything. Slugs snails worms, you name it."

PLAN

Flying Squad (Stubbs) to do Air Search for Suspect with special GO CROW! message on flying helmet.

Case 4

Co-Cheef Tec's Case (v hard, needs xtra keen beastly powers by me, hem hem)

PLAN

To detect who robbed the jewels plus the gold watch off the jackdaw and the weasel. My keen beastly ears, eyes, nose ect. tell me that jackdaw and weasel are making up fibs, just so I will find rich things for them. They hope I will say, "Da-daaah! Look at this shiny stuff I have found, are they yours by any chance, hem hem?" So then they can pretend, saying, "Oh defny, lovely, yes those are my treasures."

Yours R U kiddingly,

Your Little
Tracker

Dear Mum and Dad,

I know you like a good fib, so look at these woppers I wrote down in my notebook by shortpaw (quck wrtin):

Me (detectively): Tll me Mistr Jckdaw, whr did you hde yr jewels? Ws it in a gd hidy-hole?

Jackdaw (harshly): I tuckd ma sprkly jools nder a lmp of moss, see, and ma nest is way up top of a bell twer. So no way could any nrmal brute find it. It was a spook, I reckn.

Me (crafty): No nrmal brute, hem hem, I see. A spook, eh? Now let me ask Mr Weasel, dd you like yr gld wtch? Also, did you keep it in a daft place like on your frnt doorstp?

Weasel (front toothly): My gld watch was my best thing. It was worth a frtune. I kept it lockd in a chest hid at the btm of a deep dark

28

tunl that I dug for it spesh. No brute knew where it was, only me. It must have been stln by a soopnachrel fors. By the way can you spell s–u–p–e–r–n–a–t–u–r–a–l f–o–r–c–e?

Me (correctly): Oh, thanks. Now I cn spell it. But what Xactly is a supernatural force, hint hint?

Weasel: It is 1 of those nsty little green things that I saw come creepn into my bdrm in the drk on the bong of midnit. It was shockn. Would you like a description?

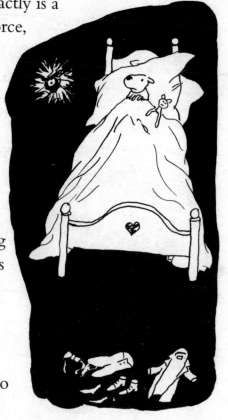

Me: Will I have to take it to the chemist?

Weasel: I said a DEscription not a PREscription.

Me: Thank you wunce morely.

Description of "not normal brute", "spook"
and "nasty thing".

Yours pulltheotheronely,

My mat with all Supercub pics on

Dear Mum and Dad,

You say stop doing that silly short writing.
Also you say my letter made you think of
Uncle Bigbad and go all sad and snappish. But
listen, why does that supernatural force
remind you of Uncle? True,
Uncle was a ghost and did
glowing in the dark. But
he was not 1 bit like the
small ratty thing that the
weasel saw floating by
his nose in the night
time. Uncle was a great
big tall horrible ghost
when he went haunting.
He had a great big horrible
furry face, plus big horrible
red eyes, plus big horrible
yellow teeth and all dribble dribbling
down. Also his eyebrows met in the middle
like Dad's only more caterpillary.

31

I know Uncle Bigbad got stolen in his whisky bottle from my house, but serves him right. He should not have scoffed so many bakebeans then he would not have died of the jumping beanbangs in the first place. And why didn't he stay in the nice grave I dug for him? He would have been safe there. He only moved into that bottle to show off, just because the label had 'Powerful Spirit' on it.

Then he got corked up and spooknapped by Mister Twister the fox.

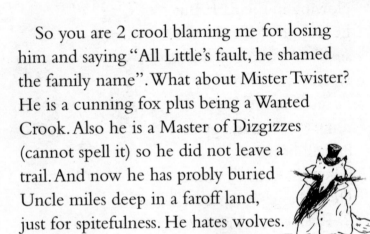

So you are 2 crool blaming me for losing him and saying "All Little's fault, he shamed the family name". What about Mister Twister? He is a cunning fox plus being a Wanted Crook. Also he is a Master of Dizgizzes (cannot spell it) so he did not leave a trail. And now he has probly buried Uncle miles deep in a faroff land, just for spitefulness. He hates wolves.

Yours suggestingly,

LB Wolf (helpful son)

Sock drawer

Dear Mum and Dad,

Your Spesh Delivery arrived today, so I got your tape recording of Dad having a fierce go at me. It was very scary, even listening in my sock drawer. I played it 2 times because 1st time I had socks stuffed 2 far up my ears.

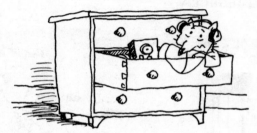

So yes, alright, I am repeating after you,

1) I am a rubbish detective and not modern enuff.
2) It is a good idea if you want to send Private Investigator Furlock Homes-Wolf.
3) Yes, I understand. He is going to do some proper investigating and find all the lost small brutes and treasure quick.

33

4) Also, he will do hi-tech investigating about Uncle Bigbad and bring him back to Frettnin Forest so he can be a proud haunter wunce more and keep up the fierce name of Wolf in Beastshire.

Plus Smells is coming on the train with him and I must be a nice big bruv to him and not put him on a lead or in a kennel or anything.

Yours sighingly,

Little

Dear Mum and Dad,

Yesterday I had to go all the way south to Badpenny Junction to meet Furlock Homes-Wolf and Smells. It was a long trot by myself round Lake Lemming and across Shocking Marshes so I was a bit late.

Yeller, Stubbs and Normus are still out looking for missing small brutes. 3 more went missing in the night: 1 otter pup, 1 small squirrel plus 1 earwiggle. Also more brute beasts came in to say they saw the small floaty green glowmouse thing in the night. And when they woke up, their treasure was robbed. But no pawprints or anything.

When I got to the station I thought blow, missed them, because the train was going away puffingly in the distance. But no, a big, fat wolf was standing there on the platform. In 1 front paw he was holding a small hard suitcase, plus Smell's ted was in the other.

What flat feet he has got! Not mentioning
what a big hat and cape plus what big glasses!
I said, "Hello you must be Mister Furlock
Homes-Wolf. I am L Wolf,
Esqwire, Number 1 cub of
Gripper. Also, Co–Cheef
Detective of the YFDA."

He said, "Did
somebody speak?"

I said, "Yes, me
down here under your
big tummy."

He said, "I knew that
actually. Wait there while I work out who you
are on my hi-tech laptop machine." Then he
opened the suitcase and went clickerty click,
keypad keypad keypad. Then he said, "Ah,
elementary my dear Spotson, you must be
Master... er... Knitting Wool."

I said, "No, I am Little Wolf" and he said,
"I knew that actually. The machine is never
wrong."

I said, "Excuse me, where is my baby bruv and why are you holding his ted's paw?"

He said, "Ted? Don't be ridiculous. Ted is on the luggage rack with my suitcase. See for yourself."

I said, "But Mister Furlock, the train left five mins ago" and he said, "I just said that actually!"

Never mind, I spect Smells will turn up in Lost Property tomorrow.

Yours tufflucky (only kidding),

Little

Dear Mum and Dad,

Me and Mister Furlock Homes-Wolf had to go all the way down to Nasty Bend today to fetch Smells from the Lost Property office there. The guardman made me pay a big fine for Smells because of him doing monkey swings on the emerjuncy string. Also pretending to be luggage (plus eating the station master's wissul).

Smells went whiny and would not walk so I had to piggyback him all the way home with the hic-wissuls. Also, I had to keep picking up Mister Furlock. He trips over a lot. (He is ~~shortsitid~~, ~~shirtseated~~, needs thick gogs).

Yeller, Normus and Stubbs were waiting for us at the YFDA, but all a bit gloomish because of not solving *any* cases or finding *any* lost small brutes.

Mister Furlock said, "Aha! That is because of you not being hi-tech. Tomorrow I shall show you sad small dim detectives some *proper* investigating." Then he ate all the supper and got his head stuck in the stewpot.

Your peckish cub,

Little Starver

Dear Mum and Dad,

Mister Homes-Wolf says we may call him Furlock now, plus he let us have a look at his special investigator power-tools.

Here is a pic to show small detectives why using your keen beastly senses is rubbish.

Technotracker™ – featuring:

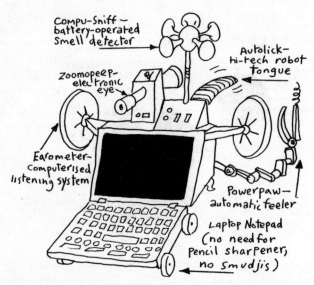

Compu-Sniff – battery-operated smell detector

Autolick – hi-tech robot tongue

zoomopeep – electronic eye

Earometer – computerised listening system

Powerpaw – automatic feeler

Laptop Notepad (no need for pencil sharpener, no smudjis)

Plus it shows Y using your animal instincts is much 2 old fash.

40

Furlock gave us a lesson on how to do automatic sniffing at dinner time. He went clickerty click keypad keypad keypad.

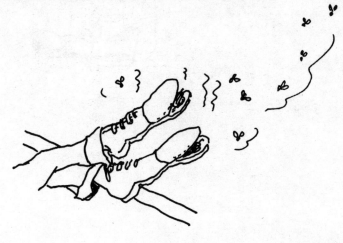

Then the machine said (robot voice), "Nasal report! You have a fine cheese on the table. Smellymentary my dear Watson."

Yeller said, "SORRY TO MENTION IT, BUT MY NOSE REPORTS THERE IS NO CHEESE ON THE TABLE, JUST YOUR FEET MISTER FURLOCK!"

Furlock said, "I knew that actually. The keys are a little sticky, that's all."

Furlock says he will do more lessons tomorrow if I pay him 3 gold coins. Handy, because that is just how many Stubbs found in Frettnin Forest the other day. Arrrooo!

Yours Xpectingalottly,

Little

Dear Mum and Dad,

Our lesson today was looking for Furlock's lost glasses. We spent 3 hours looking for them with the Technotracker. It found 1 window, some marbles, 2 jamjars and the bathroom mirror. Then Smells went har har, he had them on all the time. He likes wearing them, he says they make him go all funny and giddy.

Furlock said, "I knew that actually. Now, I think you cubs would learn a lot if I told you how I solved my most *celebrated* case, *The Case of the Slippery Chicks*. Are you familiar with it?"

Normus said, "Not really, you have only told us it 15 times."

So Furlock said good, and he told us again.

It was wunce upon a cold early spring-time. All the wolves up the hilly end of Lonesome Woods (near your lair) were starving hungry, so they prowled round looking for some tasty snacks to pounce on. Then along came a chicken with 7 chicks. But the wolves could not catch hold of the chicks to eat, they were much 2 slippery (so shaming). So they called for Mister Furlock Holmes-Wolf, Investigator, hem hem. Then off he went crawlingly through the frosty grass and soonly he came up to a chicken's nest. He pointed his machine at it. And guess what the Technotracker detected? The hen with a butterknife in her beak, spreading margarine on her babies. So he pinched her butterknife. And that was how he became a Faymuss Wolf Hero and Hi-tech Investigator. The end.

Normus did a whisper to me saying, "Hum, I could have spied that hen in just 3 secs, I bet." But Furlock said paws on lips, no talking. Then he told us about some other faymuss cases he solved. *The Case of the Polished Piggies, The Case of the Hairoiled Hares, The Case of the Soapy Snakes, The Case of the Hard to Hold Eels,* plus *The Case of the Skiddy Sausage Dogs,* ect. So boring.

Stubbs said, "Ark! Arkzactly" meaning aren't these cases arkzactly the same?"
Yeller said, "YEAH, AREN'T THEY KIND OF... IDENTICAL?"

That was when we all got donked on the head with the Technotracker.

Yours bumply,

●L Wolf.

PS Ouch.

Dear Mum and Dad,

Furlock said I could have a go with the Technotracker if I gave him xtra Moosepops at snacktime. He said, "Anyway, you had better test it out in case you damaged it with your heads yesterday."

So I went clickerty click, keypad keypad keypad and the machine said: "Hearing alert! A small mouse just crept in. It scoffed all the Moosepops and removed the turnups from Investigator Furlock's trousers."

Yeller said, " I THINK THAT MACHINE IS A BIT WRONG, BECAUSE THAT MOUSE WAS YOUR BABY BRUV."

Normus said, "Hum, have another go."

So I went clickerty click, keypad keypad keypad and the machine went, "Nasal alert! The house is on fire."

Stubbs went, "Ark! Smark" meaning Yes, I smell smark as well!

But not really, because guess what? Stubbs put furballs in Furlock's pipe, to make a cosy nest!

Yours coffingly,

PS I think the Technotracker is a bit rubbish. The YFDA are better clue hunters (true).

By the big window, staring out (Xcitedly)

Dear Mum and Dad,

Guess what? We had a circus come from Murkshire today. But then all the animals got kidnapped so no show, boo shame. I wanted to see the helifant in case it looks like a helicopter (I like flying).

CIRCUS CANCELLED

I am still hopeless at hi-tech work but here is some GOOD NEWS! You know that small moose that went missing? Stubbs found out he has come back to his herd. Arrroooo! Funny thing is, his antlers. They have gone all rubbery so not much good for butting with. Oo-er.

Yours Yzatly?

Little ??????

Dear Mum and Dad,

More good news! All the small lost brutes
have been unkidnapped, not just the snacky
1s but the fierce pouncers also.

They all said the same kind of story, like
this. A nice gingery gypsy or minty sweep or
knifegrinder came up to them and looked
into their eyes saying, softly, softly: "My boys,
you must come to my lovely dark den with
me." So they went far off from Frettnin Forest.

Then they got put in cages. Then they had
to be partners with 1 other small brute and
go into a nice big metal room. Next they had
to hold paws and do Ringa Ringa Rosie.

Plus funny sparks started shooting about. Then they all fell down. Then they could not remember. Then they came back to Frettnin Forest to live happy ever after (a tickoff by their mums and dads for talking to strangers).

Only they are not xactly the same as before. Like the ducklings. If their mum drops a plate and it goes BANG!! all the ducklings come quacking up quick saying, "Hello, we like bangs". Also the hedgehogglet has got a zip under his tummy, so now he can take off his prickles, easy cheesy. All the little rabbits say, "Maa-aa" and won't hide down their holes. Plus they want their mum to knit them white woolly jumpers.

This is funny 2. The lion cub has gone off meat, all he wants is toffee apples.

This looks like a job for THE YFDA! Arrrooo! We are soooooo xcited!

Yours petitly,

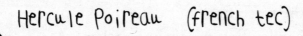

Hercule Poireau (french tec)

PS Moi really.

Dear Mum and Dad,

No, I won't let *your* darling baby pet go off on his own with any knifegrinder or minty stranger. But tell him not to be such a ~~noosence noosense~~ pain. He keeps flashing the torch from our detective kit plus handcuffing the Technotracker.

Your niggly,

Senior Boy (hem hem)

Dear Mum and Dad,

Da-daah! We have a new case!

A hermit came knocking at our door today saying, "Good day, I would like to speak to a detective."

I was just going to say, "Hello, I am Little Wolf, Co-Cheef Detective," but Furlock said buttinnly, "You are fortunate. Please enter. Allow me to introduce myself. Furlock Holmes-Wolf, celebrated Hi-Tech Investigator at your service."

The hermit came in with a wopping cloak on. He had sharp eyes, big boots plus rubber gloves. Also he smelled of catmint and his trousers were all bunchy at the back. He said (hermitly), "Good morrow. I am a just a poor old hermit. I live in a woodcutter's cottage by

myself and last night I was visited by a horrid
green spookly thing. I have nothing to rob, but
I fear I shall be kidnapped. I need protecting.
Is that part of your YFDA service?"

Furlock said, "Fear no more,
old hermit. 3 of my
young helpers, Yeller,
Normus and
Smellybreff will
protect you. I
personally shall
bring my faithful
Technotracker to
investigate the
green intruder."

Yeller said,
"GOOD, I LIKE
PROTECTIN."

Normus said, "Yes, and I like bashing
intruders."

I said, "Hey, do not forget me and Stubbs?"

So Furlock said, "Little Wolf and Stubby Crow will remain here in case of emergencies."

Then Smells started whining, saying he was not going, he hated woodcutters' huts. But then the hermit's sharp eyes went wide and he said softly, "My boy, something tells me that you are a keen young chappie who is eager to assist an old hermit in his difficulties." Smells did not know how to say no to him. So off they *all* went in a small keen pack.

Oh boo, I hate staying at home, not fair.

Yours fedduply,

Littly

Dear Mum and Dad,

Me and Stubbs waited and waited all night
but no emerjuncies for us, boo shame.

At sunjump we wanted to be busy so we ran
rushingly on the trail with our magnifying
glasses. We followed the boot and
pawprints for many a minute

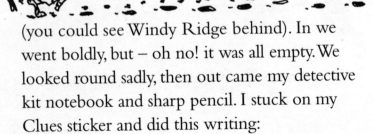

and many an hour
because it went all zigzaggy. But that
did not put us off, because after long searching
in the deep dark forest we found the woodcutter's hut in a clearing. It was just on the
north edge of Frettnin Forest,

(you could see Windy Ridge behind). In we
went boldly, but – oh no! it was all empty. We
looked round sadly, then out came my detective
kit notebook and sharp pencil. I stuck on my
Clues sticker and did this writing:

CLUES

- 🐾 1 big room, few books, big fireplace, not much ~~fernichure~~ ~~funnychir~~ chairs ect.
- 🐾 loads of rope (v sticky)
- 🐾 1 Technotracker — bashed to bits on floor
- 🐾 1 screwed up piece of paper (nothing on it)
- 🐾 large rubber gloves
- 🐾 loads of dandylion stalks with seeds blown off
- 🐾 1 of these ➡️

Then we went hurryingly outside again to look for a new trail. Stubbs did Air Searching but we could only find the trail we came by, not 1 other whiff or print! Where has everybody gone?

Yours scratchheadly,
    Little ????

57

Dear Mum and Dad,

Now the Technotracker is dead, me and Stubbs must do our detecting the good old fash way (loads of brute instinct, plus use keen beastly senses, ect. remember?).

So Stubbs unscrewed the paper. He made it nice and flat and laid it on the floor but no writing on it.

Next he started poking his clever beak into the books while I had a good sniff and lick round the room, thinking, Hmmm, all that funny rope. Y is it so thick and sticky? What is that metal thing called a HE? Y are there no fingerprints of the hermit, because I can see loads of pawprints of Furlock, Yeller, Normus and Smells?

Also I could smell all the different smells of them, plus a strong scent of catmint. I said outloudly, "Hmm, catmint, let me see..." and all of a suddenly, Stubbs said, "Ark!" meaning look what I have found in the enzarkclopedia!

He showed me how somebody had turned down the corner of 1 page, at letter C for... **catmint**. Quick as a chick, I read the words on the page:

> **Catmint:** A fine smelly plant loved by cats and other cunning pouncers. The smell is strong enough to cover up all kinds of other strong scents, including parsley, mint, rosemary, thyme and Pepper

And guess what? On the word *pepper* there was a pawprint. "That is a foxprint!" I xclaimed. Stubbs went, "Ark!" meaning arkstraordinary detecting work.

And which fox would go "Pepper! Yessss!"
And poke the word with his paw? Stubbs
went, "Ark" meaning it is arksactly the same
fox who would dress up as a gypsy, knifegrinder or hermit.

Answer: **Mister Twister!**

Smellymintery my dear parentals!

 LW

PS But which way did he go?

Dear Mum and Dad,

2 branes are better than 1, that is Y me and Stubbs are good workouters.

Stubbs went to have a good look up the chimney so I had a close look at the funny metal thing with HE on. It had a little tap on it. I gave it a turn and it went FSSSSSSHH! So scary!

But now in my notebook I write...

SOLVED MYSTERIES

<u>Who was that hermit?</u>
Answer, Mister Twister, cunning fox and master of Dizgizzes (cannot spell it) ✓

<u>Y did he have bunchy trousers at the back?</u>
Answer, to hide his bushy red tail ✓

Y rubber gloves?

Answer, to hide foxy paw-prints when thieving ✓

NOT SOLVED

🐾 Where did the sticky rope come from? ✗
🐾 How did Mister Twister get everybody out with no trail? ✗
🐾 Who blew all those dandylions? ✗
🐾 Y did he screw up a nice piece of paper with no writing or scribbuls on? ✗

Wait. Stubbs has come back down the chimney saying "Ark!" meaning he is all arkscited. Must find out Y. Will write again soonly.

Yours investigately,

Little

PS Do you know an investigator is an alligator in a vest (not really, joke to stop you going sob, where is our baby?)

On the sooty floor (undrafty bit), Woodcutter's Cottage, Frettnin Forest

Dear Mum and Dad,

Good thing Stubbs got nice and sooty because he landed on that unscrewed piece of paper and had a good shake. It was like a magic thing because letters came up on the paper! I will say Y. Because of someone (being Mister Twister) using it to lean on when he was doing heavy writing on *another* piece of paper on top. Get it? He made all dents and lines and when they got sooty they looked like this:

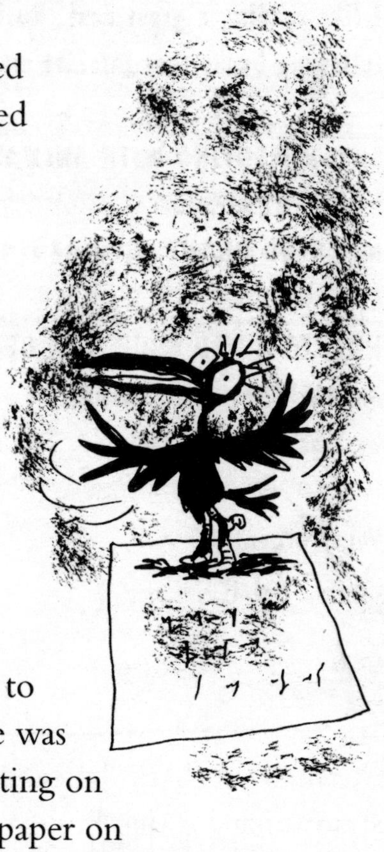

**The Hermitage, Woodcutter's Cottage,
The Clearing, Frettnin Forest, Beastshire**

My Dear Bookseller,

I like reading a great deal. Rush me the
following books that interest me strangely.

**EXPERIMENTING WITH ANIMALS
by Ken U. Altrum
MUCKING ABOUT WITH GENES
by I. M. Rich
HOW TO BUILD YOUR OWN GENETIC
MODIFICATION CHAMBER
by Ivor Startupp-Kitt**

Yours urgently,

A. Hermit

Stubbs went, "Arks" meaning
arkstraordinary, is that how you spell 'jeans'?
But we found *Genetic Modification* in the

enzarklopedia. It said it means changing
things by messing about with their insides.
That is a bit 2 hard for us, we are only small.
So *what* is that cunning fox up to?

But now, clever Stubbs has detected how
Mister Twister got away. I will say later but
Stubbs is saying "Ark!" meaning arkscuse
him. He wants me to help him quick. He is
making something with his clever beak. It is
good.

Yours bizzybeely,

Buzzy

Dear Mum and Dad,

What do you think? I am sending you this nice pic of our airship we made in the night-time. We made it out of the sticky rope, the wastepaper basket and a rubber glove blown up with FSSSSSSSH out of the metal thing with HE on. (If you turn it round it has got LIUM on its back. HE + LIUM = gas for blowing up balloons and airships! We looked that up in the enzarklopedia big book too!) Arrrooo!

Now I 'spect you will say, Little Wolf, what are you up 2 now? Answer, flying north-north-eastly on the trail of Mister Twister. But you will say, Little, do not be such a guesser. How can you tell Mister Twister went away airly? Also how can you tell which way he went?

Answer, *helium-entary* my dear Mum and Dad! Because:

1) Stubbs has done big Air Searches lately, meaning he knows the wind here is a north-north-east 1.

2) He found loads of pawprints going just 1 way.

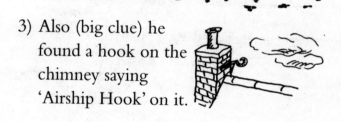

3) Also (big clue) he found a hook on the chimney saying 'Airship Hook' on it.

4) He found loads more dandylions with the seeds blown off. That was a hard puzzle but we did a shut-your-eyes-and-think-squeezingly. All of a suddenly, Stubbs said, "Ark!" meaning eurarka, I have found out something!

I said, "What?" Answer. Mister Twister was holding up dandylion clocks to find out *how* strong the wind was blowing and *which way*! So well done our Flying Squad!

Your breezy boy,

L W

PS Hmm, flying. Lovely.

Dear Mum and Dad,

We have landed bonkingly near Broken Tooth Caves. Stubbs wanted to let all the FSSSSSH out with a sharp peck. But I said no, save it for later. So we hid the airship behind a big rock. Now it is v dark, but Stubbs is holding the torch in his clever beak so I can do my writing. A good job we had our detective kit with us.

The paths round here are rocky, so no pawprints, but we found 1 good clue:

This is a button off Smells's sailor suit, so he is probably kidnapped and in a cave. With the others, I bet. BUT (big but) which cave? There are many!

It is creepy here. My beastly instinct has gone all tickly like when I see a big hairy spider. There must be lots of spiders very close by.

Ooooooooooooooooooooo!

What was that? A loud trumpet noise! Sorry about smudje. All quiet now. We are starving. Wish I had 1 of Mum's rabbit rolls or a tasty mice pie yum yum. I will have to look for emerjuncy rations instead.

Yours rummagingly,

Littly

Behind a big rock, by Broken Tooth Caves, Dark Hills

Dear Mum and Dad,

Did I say we were both starving hungry and wishing for Mum's rabbit rolls yum yum? Well I got out my emerjuncy matchbox to see if I had any tasty crawlers in it for crunchy snacks. It was empty, boo shame. So out with our magnifying glasses and off we went searchingly in the crooks and nannies. (Other way round, sorry.)

We searched and searched. My yellow eyes made friends with the dark but then

HELP!

TYRANOSAURUS

REX!

Yours hoppitly,

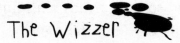
The Wizzer

Dear Mum and Dad,

You want to go careful with magnifying glasses. Sometimes they do tricks to trick you, because you know that T-rex? It was a stick insect really. The magnifying glass was just pretending.

Never mind because, guess what? The stick insect jumped in my match box. So handy! I was just going to give it a nibble but Stubbs said, "Ark", meaning that is arkstraordinary! Y did the stick insect just hop in your matchbarks like that?

So I said, "Tell me, Mister Crunchy Snack, how did you learn to do hopping so high?" And the insect said (stickly), "I learned it off of a cricket. I had to hold hands with him and do a Ringa Ringa Rosie in the metal room that went all sparky."

I said, "Oo-er, I have heard that Ringa Ringa Rosie story before. Were you by any chance captured by a foxy hermit? Or a minty knifegrinder? Or a gingery gypsy?"

The sticky said back, "Yes I was! But I..." Stubbs said, "Ark!" meaning, you arkscaped.

The sticky said, "Cor what a clever cub and crowchick you are. You should be detectives."

I said a proud aha. "Aha we *are* detectives. We are from the YFDA. And that foxy kidnapper was none other than Mister Twister, master of dizzgizzes (cannot spell it) and wanted crook of Frettnin Forest. Now tell us what happened because I am always ready, and my pencil is a sharp 1."

Yours notingly,

Dear Mum and Dad,

We have made friends with Sticky, he is nice and a good watcher so no eating him. (Lucky Stubbs shared his wiggly grubs with me, so my tummy is not 2 rumbly now.) Sticky says he has seen lots of cages here. They are full of captured brute beasts, some big, some small. All sorts. The biggest 1 is grey, like a big wrinkly house with 4 legs. It has ears like car doors, plus a hosepipe in the front for tunes and hoovering you up. Praps that is the helifant that got kidnapped from the circus. Praps it was him made us jump with his loud trumpet.

Also, Sticky says, sometimes Mister Twister carries a whisky bottle. He holds it up like a lantern when he goes walking in the dark tunnels and looking in the cages. He says it shines with a green glow. Oh no, I think that green glowness is the ghost of Uncle Bigbad! So shaming to end up as a lamp for a fox!

1 other bad thing is, Mister Twister has got 2 terrible creatures to guard the cages all the time. They are big as cats and fierce with 8 furry legs like spiders! They made all that sticky rope, I bet! No wonder my fur feels tickly all the time. Spiders are my worst thing ('cept for loud bangs).

Sticky told us that the last things Mister Twister captured were 4 cocoons, like silkworms. 1 was a big, fat cocoon. Another was big and furry. 1 was small and loud. Then there was a small 1 with a sailor hat on. That is Furlock, Normus, Yeller and Smells I bet. Captured by the hermit. Sticky says they are locked up in the Hall of Cages, near the metal room that goes sparky, and guarded by spidercat guards.

Sticky wants to come rescuing with us. He wants to save his chum the cricket. Because he cannot jump away himself. Good eh?

Stubbs said, "Ark!" meaning do not worry, we will help the crarket to arkscape!

Pawscrossly for luck,

 Little cheef

Dear Mum and Dad,

We are in Broken Tooth Caves. It is drippy and ploppy and so much tunnels. But Sticky has good feelers for finding the way in the darkness. We must not use Stubby's torch, 2 giveaway, so I am writing this in glowworm juice. Hope U can read it.

Wait. We have found the Hall of Cages. It is quiet. We can hear small snores. That is a mouse snore. That is a badger. A ferret, a squirrel. Tippy on the toes. Wait. My nose is telling me. Yes! I smell a baby bruv. He is near. I must use my keenly senses. Wish my yellow eyes were *more* keen.

Ooo-er! There is Smells in his little cocoon –
very still, no wiggling! Also Yeller, Normus
and Furlock all stuck up tight. And such a big
lock on the cage door.

Oh no, help! Stubbs has got pounced on!

Yours panickly,

By a plughole

Dear Mum and Dad,

It was Mister Twister's Spidercat
Guards! Huge miaowing spiders – help!
They came swinging from the roof on
their sticky ropes. Stubbs gave 1 a hard peck but
they were 2 strong and tied him up spinningly.

Up went my fur, all tickly on my back. That
was my beastly instinct saying 2 me, *Look out
behind you, Little!* I went flat but then Stubbs
called "Ark!"meaning fire arkstinguisher! It
was just by me on the wall.

Bang I went on the button and out came
the water with a SHUSHHHHH! Har har,
that was a good hard skwirter. I shouted, "Put
your legs up, you Spidercats! I am a proud

79

detective wolf, so you are under arrest. Give
me the keys to the cages."

They tried to pounce
on me swiftly. So I
skwirted and
skwirted them
right in the nasty
eyes and right in
the nasty teeth. I
chased them along the
Hall of Cages till they came
to a big drainhole and DOWN they went

wooshingly. And guess
what? The keys
dropped out of
their horrible
mouths!

Yours servumrightly,

Sir Skwirtalot Wolf

Dear Mum and Dad,

I got the penknife out of my Detective Kit
and cut Stubbs free. Then we unlocked the
cage and Stubbs got busy with his clever
beak. All the sticky rope was in heaps on the
floor before you could say a kwick thing like,
"Hello everybody, we have come to save you".

Yeller said, "WELL DONE LITTLE AND
STUBBS." But Smells gave me a sharp nip
because he likes
being tied up.
And Furlock
said, "I knew
you would
come actually. Did
you find us by my Technotracker?"

I said, "No we found you by our eyes, noses
and other beastly senses, because we are the
YFDA. And the Technotracker is defnly a
TechNOtracker now. It was Mister Twister
who did smashing up."

81

He said, "What? Did you say *smashing up*? TSO! TSO! Quick!"

Normus said, "What is TSO – is it bashing?"

Furlock said, "TSO is Trot Swiftly Off! NOW!"

I said, "But we have nearly found out WHODUNNIT and WOTFOR. And we have to rescue Uncle Bigbad's ghost. And what about freeing the other brute beasts and arresting Mister Twister?"

Furlock said, "Frankly, I do not care a flea WHODUNNIT or WOTFOR, or for Bigbad Wolf either. He is far too wild for my liking. I intend to TSO before anyone thinks of smashing *me* up. If you have any sense, you will join me while you still can. Goodbye. Whoops." And off he rushed, trippingly. He was only wurrid about saving himself. Oh blow.

Yours leftinthelurchly,

 THE YFDA

Dear Mum and Dad,

Pity about Furlock, eh? Ask Dad to give him a good nip next time he sees him.

Yeller said, "GOOD RIDDANCE TO HIM! AND WELL DONE, CHUMS! YOU SAVED US. THAT CRAFTY FOX WAS GOIN TO EXPERIMENT ON US TODAY. HE WAS GOIN TO PUT US IN HIS METAL ROOM. HE SAID WE ARE THE LAST PART OF HIS CUNNIN PLAN."

Normus said, "Yes, well done fellers! Now we can do some bashing at last!"

I said, "No bashing yet, Normus. 1st we must find out Mister Twister's cunning plan. Where is he?"

Yeller said, "HE IS IN A LOCKED ROOM TALKIN INTO HIS TAPE RECORDER."

I said, "Then we must use our keenly senses to find out what he is saying."

Normus said, "Shame we haven't got an electronic listening device like Furlock had. We could bug the room with that."

That made Yeller have 1 of his Big Ideers. He said, "BUG–AMENTARY MY DEAR NORMUS! WE **WILL** PUT A BUG INTO LISTEN. BUT NO NEED FOR ELECTRIC!"

Sticky said bravely, "I'm a bug. Will I do?" but Stubbs said, "Ark!" meaning, what about your friend the craket? He would be even better.

Time for Hunt the Cricket. Arrroooo!

Yours eagerly,

The YFDA

Dear Mum and Dad,

It did not take long finding the cricket, he was in a jamjar close by. He was a bit wurrid in case of getting scoffed, but then he was happy to be a detective bug for us.

We went shushly along the dark Hall of Cages. Soonly we found a big strong door saying TOP SECRET– CRAFTY FOXES ONLY! Quick as a chick we popped the cricket in the keyhole, so he could see and hear that cunning crook and kidnapper Mister Twister. Plus he could talk to us, by rubbing his legs together chirpingly. Good eh?

Yours spyly,

 Little Eye

Dear Mum and Dad,

Here is the cricket news (translated by Sticky, he speaks cricket best). This was spoken softly into a tape recorder by Mister Twister about his secret Xperiments!

"**Crafty Plan, Code Name PYOF. Listening Diary of My Crafty Self, Day 43.** Testing, testing. Hello, dear boy. As I speak today, my Master Plan is almost complete, so I shall give myself the pleasure of summing up my *remarkable* achievement. My first brilliant stroke was to kidnap my rival in crime, the once great and terrible Bigbad Wolf. The label on the whisky bottle where he resides reads 'Powerful Spirit'. What nonsense that seems, for now – ha ha – he is my pet, my slave. And why must he do all that I command? Simple!

"The answer is pinned to my chest. It is a well known fact that he who dares to snatch a single hair from the tail of a wolf shall master him forever – and I have his entire *tail*! How? I hear you cry! By craft and cunning, for I knew that the wretch had blown himself to pieces as a result of eating bakebeans too fast. I also discovered that the only part of him that his pesky nephew, Little Wolf, could find to bury was his whiskers. So patiently I searched and snuffed, never giving up until I had tracked down the tail that has made my fortune!

"Knowing that ghosts can always find hidden stores of gold and jewels, my first command to him was to keep his miniature shape and size, and to do all my treasure seeking. That allowed me time to kidnap at least 1 small brute of every species in Frettnin Forest. And to study.

87

"Very soon I taught my sharp self the science of genetic modification, for I wished to change the kidnapped creatures for the *better*. Better for me, that is! My aim was to turn them into *convenience food*! Once Bigbad had stolen enough treasure to allow me to do so, I purchased a beautiful machine – my metal box – my Genetic Modification Chamber! After that, I began my Great Plan, **Code Name PYOF!** It has been a huge success and is almost complete. I am switching off now in order to carry our my final Master Stroke!"

Oh no, he is coming out.....

Yours hidingly,

Dear Mum and Dad,

Back we all went gaspingly to the Hall of Cages. Cricket's legs were stiff from so much chirping, but we all had to use our keenly beastly senses quick! This is our plan:

1) Sticky and Cricket – take keys and open up all the cages
2) Me and Stubbs – hide high up in the shadows
3) Normus, Yeller and Smells – pretend to be tied up again in their cage (Smells likes that part)
4) Get a big, fat sack so it looks like Furlock is in the cage 2.

I will tell you the rest if it works.

Yours riskingly,

 L Wolf

PS If not, goodbye forever, Mum and Dad. We tried our best. Call out the Murkshire Wolf Pack and get ready to have a fight against Mister Twister before he gets you 2.

Dear M and D,

Not dead, but nearly, phew. I will say what happened:

Up lit the hall with the green glow of Uncle Bigbad. Mister Twister was holding Uncle up by his bottle to light the way. He was speaking into his tape recorder again, saying softly:

"Listening Diary, Day 43, continued. As I was saying before I interrupted myself, my Master Plan is to turn Frettnin Forest into a **PYOF** or **Pounce on Your Own Forest**! I shall soon be able to feast on all my favourite creatures with *no danger to myself whatsoever*! My prey will be easy and my enemies will be feeble and powerless against me! I shall grow gorgeously fat and sleek and never have a single worry.

"Using my GM chamber, I have mixed up the shapes and habits of my kidnap victims, large and small.  Already I have created a vegetarian lion by crossing him with a baa–lamb. I have crossed a pheasant with a gun–dog, so that it runs towards hunters with shotguns. I have crossed a hedgehog with a washbag so that I can unzip his prickles and have a deliciously instant snack. A piggy has been crossed with a rabbit so that he will pop straight into the cooking pot, crying 'Lucky me, I have found my burrow!' A shy little  mouse has been crossed with a hyena so now I can hear him laughing, no matter how tall the grass is where he hides.

"One by one I am returning these changed creatures to their homes. Only yesterday I sent back a young squirrel. His mother is wondering why he is terrified of heights and will not climb up to his dray. She has no idea that I have crossed him with a mole!

"Now, as a special treat for myself, I have saved the best experiment till last. I intend to cross some meddling wolves and an interfering young bear with a litter of poodle pups. After just 30 seconds playing Ring-a-Ring-a-Roses in my GM Chamber, they will all be tamed. They will roll over on their backs and let me tickle their tummies! Spidercat guards bring out the prisoners!"

Help!
Yours tobecontinuedly,

The proud cubs
of Frettnin Forest

Dear M and D,

Har har, hee hee, I love having my tummy tickled by a crafty fox (not really, only kidding).

We had a nice BIG shock for Mister Twister. Me and Stubbs were The Flying Squad. We came dropping quick out of the roof shadows. Down we whooshed swingingly on a sticky rope. I put out my paws like an X and Stubbs sat on my head and made an X with his legs and wings. So when Mister Twister saw our shadow coming, he thought we were a Spidercat guard!

Then Yeller gave his war howl – ARROOOOOOOOO! He and Normus

and Smells threw their ropes off, opened their
cage and charged snappingly at the vain and
peppery plotter. Mister Twister tried to bash
them with his tape recorder, but I kept
swinging and knocked him over with a flying
kick. That was when Stubbs grabbed Uncle
Bigbad's whisky bottle in his clever beak and
flew away with it.

And guess what I
got with my clever paw?
Uncle's tail!

Sticky and Cricket were good unlockers.
Out came all the kidnapped creatures
chargingly. They butted and pecked and
bashed and bit and gave that fox a good noisy
fight. The helifant made his scariest trumpet
noise and did a lot of nice squashing and
squishing and swishing with his hosepipe. He
was sooooo Xcited to be out of his cage!

95

But he lost his way in the darkness and got himself stuck in the GM Chamber, boo shame.

That made Mister Twister get his cunningness up again. He turned his foxy eyes on us saying, "Now my boys, stop all this roughness. Just look deep deeeep into my eyes and do what I command." Good thing my brute instinct called out to Stubbs, "Quick! Throw the whisky bottle to the helifant." So he did a swift loop the loop. Then the helifant's hosepipe reached up and sucked the bottle out of his beak. I banged the door shut and switched the switch, click.

The Chamber started to shake and spark and rock as the helifant did Ringa Ringa Rosie with the ghost of Uncle Bigbad. Then

BLAM!

The Chamber door flew off and

CRACKLE FLASH FUME

Out came flying the faymuss Terror of
Haunted Hall. It was the good old
ghost of Uncle Bigbad, back to
his normal monster size! He
had his great big horrible red
eyes and his great big horrible
yellow teeth and all his horrible
dribble dribbling down. Arrrooooo!

Yours victori–ussly,

The YFDA

PS I have done a nice pic of
Mister Twister with a
bashed up tail and
lots of lumps
running away
limply.

Dear Mother and Father of mine (posh, eh?),

I ~~reseaved~~ ~~receeved~~ ~~received~~ got your letter saying Furlock came round to the Lair going moan groan, no more hi-tech investigating for him. He is opening a sticking plaster shop for sad wolves that keep tripping up and bumping their knees. And it is all my fault.

You say I am a bad boy because I did not let Smells do handcuffing on Mister Twister, he wanted to do that spesh. So now he is all upset. Also you say I must spoil your darling baby ~~pest~~ pet more, like letting him get cubnapped and tied up more often because those are his favourites. You say let him have loads more ruff fun and give in to him all the time, it is the only way.

Har har, I know that is just your wolfly way
to say well done, and pat pat for cunningness.

Also you mean to say congratarrooshuns
for solving loads of tricky cases all in 1 go by
trying hard plus normal wolfly sense and
brute instinct. Plus doing all that rescuing and
saving Frettnin Forest from being a Pounce
on Your Own Forest for one fat fox.

You are sooo nice, hem hem joke.

Yours proud Co-Cheefly,

Moi (French)

My office, a long time later

Dear Mum and Dad,

Since my last letter, The YFDA has done a lot of genetic unmodification on the kidnapped brute beasts that got put in the Chamber. Because we want Frettnin Forest back to its normal wild self. Also we wanted Uncle to go back to his proper happy haunting ground and keep up the terrible name of Wolf. Arrroooo! (I have given him back his tail but, guess what? Ssshhh, I kept 1 small hair, just in case I need to boss him about. Because then if me, Yeller and Normus want to be pirates or spacecubs, he might come in handy, yesss?)

Your busy boy,

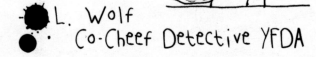

L. Wolf
Co-Cheef Detective YFDA

No, Mum and Dad, I do not mean be like peabugs. This is your invitaysh to come and see our mini circus, it is a BIG THRILL!

I have done you a pic of SMELLYBREFF
THE CLOWN doing a skwirt with his
HELIFANTEDDY. He made the helifant do
Ringa Ringa Rosie with his ted, before we
put wheels on the GM Chamber and turned
it into a nice caravan, cosy hmmmm.

Sticky and Cricket wanted to stay being
modified, so now they can be THE
AMAZING JUMPING TINY T-REX and
HIS FRIEND THE CRICKET ON STILTS.

The helifant likes being shrunk best 2.
Good because he is a nice attraction.
He can play his trumpet and
also be THE WORLD'S
ONLY HELIFANT IN
A BOTTLE.

Also we have got THE
WORLD'S LOUDEST RING
MASTER YELLER WOLF!
And Normus is our
STRONGEST
BEARCUB EVER!

Me and Stubbs are trapezers called THE
FLYING SPIDERCATS.

We are brill, come and have a thrill.

Yours swingingly,

Little Bigtop

ARROOOOOOOOO!!!

Little Wolf's Book of Badness

Ian Whybrow, illustrated by Tony Ross

All Little Wolf wants to do is stay at home with Mum, Dad and baby brother Smellybreff. Instead, he is packed off to Cunning College to learn the 9 Rules of Badness and earn a Gold BAD Badge from his wicked Uncle Bigbad. He sets off on his journey, sending letters home as he adventures in the big bad world.

'Little Wolf ranks among the most engaging animal characters in modern children's writing.' *She*

ISBN 0 00 675160 1

An *imprint* of HarperCollins*Publishers*

Little Wolf's Diary of Daring Deeds

Ian Whybrow, illustrated by Tony Ross

Little Wolf and his cousin Yeller decide that BADNESS is out, and ADVENTURES are in. But their first mistake is thinking that they can buy adventures. Their second mistake is to reply to Mister Marvo's advert for Instant Adventures (Scary but Safe). The result is that they find themselves caught up in a *real* adventure. But Little is scared of bangs; snow gives Yeller the trembles; their new friend Stubbs, the crow, is too frit to fly and… Smellybreff gets cubnapped!

'A howlingly funny book for all the family to get their teeth into.' *Young Telegraph*

ISBN 0 00 675252 7

An imprint of HarperCollinsPublishers

Little Wolf's Postbag

Ian Whybrow, illustrated by Tony Ross

ARRROOOO!

Calling all readers of Wolf Weekly. Guess who is going to be your new problem page agony nephew? Me. I am Little Wolf really, but you must pretend not knowing. Say 'Dear Mister Helpful' if you want to get a reply printed all poshly in this faymus mag. Because Mister Helpful is my nom de prune (French). So go on, what is up with you? Write quick!

ISBN 0 00 675451 1

Collins

An imprint of HarperCollins*Publishers*

Little Wolf's Handy Book of Peoms

Ian Whybrow, illustrated by Tony Ross

Dear reader, this is not a letter,

This is a peom (they are posher and better).

Don't say you hate peoms, 'cause I've done a load,

Sum are a bit rubbish, but not this wun any road,

Also I have done sum nice wuns about Mum & Dad,

So go on, have a small read, or I will get sad.

Yours rimbling rumbling rhyming-lee, from

Little Wolf, your Number 1 cub-bee.

ISBN 0 00 711904-6

Collins

An imprint of HarperCollinsPublishers

Little Wolf Pack Leader

Ian Whybrow, illustrated by Tony Ross

When Spoiler Snarl-Wolfington, posh cub and Top Wolf, forms the Murkshire RHYWP (Really Harsh Young Wolf Pack), Little Wolf is determined *not* to join. He has his own chums, and together with Normus Bear, Stubby Crow, Yeller and Smellybreff, he forms the Beastshire SPOBBTHALOF (Small Pack Of Brute Beasts That Have A Load Of Fun). Spoiler's pack are determined to capture Mr Twister and claim the huge reward (so shaming) so Little and his friends must come up with a cunning plan…

ISBN 0 00 711860 0

Collins

An imprint of HarperCollinsPublishers

Order Form

To order direct from the publishers, just make a list of the titles you want and fill in the form below:

Name ....

Address ....

....

....

Send to: Dept 6, HarperCollins Publishers Ltd, Westerhill Road, Bishopbriggs, Glasgow G64 2QT.

Please enclose a cheque or postal order to the value of the cover price, plus:

UK & BFPO: Add £1.00 for the first book, and 25p per copy for each additional book ordered.

Overseas and Eire: Add £2.95 service charge. Books will be sent by surface mail but quotes for airmail despatch will be given on request.

A 24-hour telephone ordering service is available to holders of Visa, MasterCard, Amex or Switch cards on 0141- 772 2281.

Collins

An imprint of HarperCollins*Publishers*